Breakfast at
BLOOMINGDALE'S

KRISTEN KEMP

Scholastic Press
New York

COPYRIGHT © 2007 BY KRISTEN KEMP. ALL RIGHTS RESERVED. PUBLISHED BY
SCHOLASTIC PRESS, A DIVISION OF SCHOLASTIC INC., *PUBLISHERS SINCE 1920.*
SCHOLASTIC, SCHOLASTIC PRESS, AND ASSOCIATED LOGOS ARE TRADEMARKS
AND/OR REGISTERED TRADEMARKS OF SCHOLASTIC INC. NO PART OF THIS
PUBLICATION MAY BE REPRODUCED, STORED IN A RETRIEVAL SYSTEM, OR
TRANSMITTED IN ANY FORM OR BY ANY MEANS, ELECTRONIC, MECHANICAL,
PHOTOCOPYING, RECORDING, OR OTHERWISE, WITHOUT WRITTEN PER-
MISSION OF THE PUBLISHER. FOR INFORMATION REGARDING PERMISSION,
WRITE TO SCHOLASTIC INC., ATTENTION: PERMISSIONS DEPARTMENT,
557 BROADWAY, NEW YORK, NY 10012.

LIBRARY OF CONGRESS CATALOGING-IN-PUBLICATION DATA
KEMP, KRISTEN. BREAKFAST AT BLOOMINGDALE'S/ KRISTEN KEMP   P.   CM.
SUMMARY: ALONE IN NEW YORK, SIXTEEN-YEAR-OLD CAT IS DETERMINED TO
REALIZE THE DREAM SHE SHARED WITH HER RECENTLY-DECEASED GRANDMOTHER
—TO BE A FASHION DESIGNER WHOSE LINE IS SOLD IN BLOOMINGDALE'S—
BUT FIRST SHE MUST SURVIVE THE BIG CITY AND AVOID BEING STOPPED
BY HER MOTHER.
ISBN-13: 978-0-439-80987-0   ISBN-10: 0-439-80987-8
[1. FASHION DESIGN—FICTION. 2. RUNAWAYS—FICTION. 3. GRIEF—
FICTION. 4. NEW YORK (N.Y.)—FICTION.]   I. TITLE.
PZ7.K3056BRE 2007 [FIC]—DC22   2006033217
12 11 10 9 8 7 6 5 4 3 2 1   7 8 9 10 11/ 0
PRINTED IN THE U.S.A.   23
FIRST EDITION, AUGUST 2007
THE TEXT TYPE WAS SET IN GARAMOND BOOK.
THE DISPLAY TYPE WAS SET IN GARAMOND
LIGHT CONDENSED AND LINOSCRIPT.
BOOK DESIGN BY MARIJKA KOSTIW

To Johan

Part 1
IT STARTS WITH A DEATH.

This is Chapter One.

"As most of you know, my grandmother and I were like conjoined twins — so what if we were fifty-eight years apart."

I am speaking from a wooden pulpit with a thick layer of shellac. Through a funeral haze, I smile, and I raise my index and middle fingers, pretending they're glued together. I am wearing Nina's black satin gloves that go all the way to my elbows.

I'm not nervous. Nope. Not one bit.

"If we *had* been conjoined, it would not have been at our heads or hips. Instead, it would've been at our hands. We both *lived* to sew." I am hoping my speech doesn't suck as much as I think it does. It's my first eulogy, and it's dreadful. "Wait, I guess if we were physically connected, then drawing patterns — not to mention cutting them — would've been quite difficult. But you know what I mean. We would've worked it out. We worked everything out." I sigh because I am sucking. Then I shoot a dagger glare at my mother, who is shaking her head in disapproval as usual. It's not like she's the one up here.

I won't let that mother heifer of mine get to me. I continue, "So, metaphorically, Nina and I were connected at the inseams." I point to the inside of my knee, which is bare because I'm wearing a short black dress. I hate panty hose except for fishnets, which would hardly be appropriate on this depressing sunny Friday in July. It's clear outside, but I'm stormy inside. My smile is big, and I remain painfully cheerful. No one here — including myself — could handle me right now if I got real.

People's mouths and eyes are shaped like sideways question marks, telling me they are confused. Oh, well. This isn't really for them.

The eruption of red roses, pink carnations, and orange orchids makes the room seem even smaller and more crowded. People like — I mean *liked* — my Nina. She was their personal expert seamstress and stylist — always fixing their clothes, creating new ones, and tossing in surprise accessories like leather clutches and arm warmers just for fun. She worked mostly for free — nothing I ever said could get her to charge, not in money at least. Instead, we rarely had to pay in local restaurants, bars, hair salons, or tattoo parlors. She was adored in our small upstate town

3

for her skills, her fashion tips, and the awesome all-ages parties she'd been throwing since she was twenty-one. Before that, like when she was my age, she lived in Hell's Kitchen in New York City, and we'd been planning to go back there ASAP. As soon as I finished this pesky rite of passage called high school — which I was going to do early — she and I were supposed to set off.

Well, maybe. She said she'd only go if she were still alive.

My shoulders are so heavy.

"Upstate New York will be totally boring without her." I continue my off-the-glove speech with the clear and steady voice Nina taught me to use because she believed in girl power. I go on: "We'll all miss her daily premonitions — she swore her dreams came true. Like the time her favorite kitty — rest in peace, little Truman — spoke to her in her sleep and told her not to drive the next day. Turned out that the blizzard of '02 hit full force right when she was supposed to be getting her hair dyed. Her dreams saved her life — and many of ours."

I change the subject: "And Nina had the goods,

too — you all know what I'm talking about. When I say our town of Queensbury will be boring without her, I totally mean it. Just think, who else in our midst made out with Frank Sinatra, Tommy Hilfiger, *and* Steven Tyler? Not all at once, of course." My voice is crisp, and my smile is almost genuine with memories. The water behind my eyes is genuine, too. I make those tears just dry up. *Just. Dry. Up.*

I pause. People stare like they hadn't been gossiping about Nina for all of her seventy-one years. My boyfriend breaks the silence with a forced laugh, a nice save as usual. Others go "heh, heh, heh" just to be polite.

I'm having trouble conveying that Nina was my everything — my best friend, my sewing mentor, my fashion design coach, my clothing company partner, my emotional Internet connection, my daily dining buddy. She could order some mean Chinese and Thai food — the spicier the better. I don't know how to put a lifetime of feelings into silly things like words. I only know how to put my feelings into fabric. I am imagining a simple drape, an emotional silhouette, on a long gray chiffon dress. Anyway, I don't know how to speak in public since I always skip school on oral report days. It's not that I'm scared or introverted as much as I'm afraid of sounding stupid.

But here I go, anyway, adding another attempt at lightheartedness: "If it hadn't been for her, I would be dead, and I'm not being dramatic — my mother's cooking could kill anybody." I think the joke is funny but that could be because my boyfriend and I had champagne for breakfast, in Nina's honor, and now it's only eleven A.M.

My mother heifer's current live-in fiancé, Russ, pipes in, muffling my hiccup, "I'll raise a glass to that." What a wino.

I get a laugh this time, but it's once again obligatory and uncomfortable. "Heh, heh, heh," they say. So for the next few minutes, I just play it straight about how she was sweet, thoughtful, and one-of-a-kind — the standard eulogy stuff. No one here could possibly understand the real her, anyway.

Or me without her.

I keep going, saying anything I can think of to fill the space. My voice is still clear, not choppy or breaking: "She taught me to drive when I was eleven." I straighten my shoulders — on most days I have decent posture because I am short. With my black satin-gloved hands, I pull down my black Audrey Hepburn/Holly Golightly/*Breakfast at Tiffany's*–style sleeveless shift with the above-the-knee hem I made for this occasion. I am into this dress and, *note to self,* I should make it in all the mod colors. She'd like that. I smile again because people in the audience look sad, and I take that to mean that they care. Maybe this will cheer them up: "We created patterns from Prada clothes when I was thirteen. She educated me on cool music. Her favorites were Billie Holiday, Madonna, and the Misfits." Muddy, my boyfriend, cues her favorite Madonna song, "Beautiful Stranger." "She was special. She will be missed." I bow my head as if I'm about to cry, which I am.

7

Keep it together, I tell myself as I step off the stage and count to three. My mother steps on.

"Nina would appreciate your love and support," she says, as if she were the one presiding and not me. Hmph. I'd get my nose, eyes, cheeks, and hair all pulled out and rebuilt in an artificial heartbeat so I could look like anyone but her. But that would involve knives and blood — not my favorite things. My mother heifer continues, "My daughter put this program together herself, which is why she hasn't had time to fix her hair or wax her eyebrows. Thank you again. Oh, and I know I've said it before, but please, everyone keep supporting our family by buying drip coffeemakers. Nina would appreciate it. A portion of the proceeds, of course, goes to the Pilgrim Psychiatric Center." (That's where she works.)

She always undermines me. I want to scratch her with this jagged fingernail on my middle finger, but she's not even worth taking my gloves off for. I don't tell the crowd that *someone* had to do this funeral service. I don't tell the crowd that it would never be *her.* She has a reputation. They know she's a shrink and a fruit loop. She's super-duper into abnormal psych and drip coffeemakers. She's one of those moms who never really wanted to be a mom, resenting me from binky to first bra to now. She passed me off to my grandmother and went her own way.

After my speech, people come up to me and hug and kiss and sniffle. I don't cry — like ever — especially not in public. I just hug them because they want to feel better. The tattoo artist named Kenneth, who kisses like a robot, tells me I'll be okay, then wisely runs off. *I won't.* My mother's second and third husbands remind me how much kinder Nina was than my mother. *I know.*

I don't hug my ex-best friend Madeleine Baker when she tells me in a deliberately overexaggerated way that she is "*so so SO* severely sorry" for my loss. *She's not.* Why did she even come? That prom queen/cheerleader captain mule has single-handedly made my high school life hell. She's probably only here to flirt with my boyfriend. He's her ax — I mean *ex*.

She's sugar substitute sweet in her fitted pink tweed two-piece suit. But I can't be.

I look into her soulless sparkling gray eyes then at her hair. She needs new highlights; they looked so much better when I did them for her. "Back off," I say. "The only way you belong here is in a casket of your own." I say this supercasually. The blades in my voice come out sharper.

"Harsh." Her suit is tailored just so-so. "Bitch," she mouths. She takes off before I can respond.

My mother comes up next, crying. *Sniffle, snort, blubber.* "I only made that hair-removal comment because I was jealous. Jealous of you and Nina. Of the time you two spent together. It was passive-aggressive behavior. I need to be accountable for it."

Oh, please. When Nina was alive she went out of her way to spend about five minutes a month with either of us. Yes, I technically lived with Mother and Russ, but I stayed with Nina most of the time. Not because Nina had a fabulous turn-of-the-century Victorian mansion on Mockingbird Street with a Jacuzzi, party room, and three huge spaces we turned into sewing parlors on the light-drenched first floor. I stayed because Nina loved me a lot more than this poor excuse for a maternal unit did. Tears? *Oh, please, times two.* My mother's crying because Nina's gone, and Nina gave her money. Nina is — *I mean was* — rich. Super rich. Filthy rich. Stinking rich. But she only behaved bourgeois when she threw parties and got dressed. The rest had to be normal — way too normal, if you ask me. Nina and I cleaned the house, brushed the cat before it rested in peace, washed the clothes, and even hung them out on her clothesline on beautiful days like today. She never wanted me to be anything but normal.

"You know, I believe honesty is the only way at all times," Mother Heifer says to me as she roots through the clutch purse that clashes so badly with her pleated pants.

"So are you trying to tell me you're sorry?" I ask. We are nearing the exit doors, not quite outside the funeral home.

"I'm *accountable*." She huffs away before I get a chance to get accountable right back at her. We have our reasons for not getting along, like the fact she continually abandons me for men. Nina always tried to get me to go easier on her because there's a long line of mental disorders on her father's side of the family — I mean, Great-grandma Margie had a pet coconut she kept on a leash. But Mother is a shrink, and she *knows* exactly what her issues are. She self-medicates by medicating others who are far more gone than she (typical of shrinks). Knock on whatever, I seem to be healthy in the head so far, yet I live in fear every day that I'll wake up like her.

I murmur a curse word, but I won't be murmuring much longer. I'll be using vocal cords. Nina isn't around to make us act related anymore, and she's not around to *tsssk* at my potty mouth. I can't keep pretending. My mother is mean.

Next up to greet me is Nina's neighbor, the

11

awesome interior designer. Then comes our hairstylist from Saratoga Springs. Next is Gus, the retired weatherman. Finally, Nina's Latin Gardener God shows up. There are many others, so very many others. I clench my jaws, grinding them together to make the room stop spinning. Meanwhile, the flower explosion, the ugly carpet, Kleenex boxes, and people's question-mark faces close in on me. As I head toward the exit for fresh parking lot air, Maynard Baker, the undertaker, pats my head — I tell him to be careful with the pony-tails — and says I did a pretty decent job of planning this whole thing, considering my age and education.

I'm getting ready to tell Maynard that even though I just technically finished my junior year, I'm only two classes short of graduation. But suddenly, emotions — anger, sorrow, loneliness, sadness, shame, anxiety, guilt, and more anger — paralyze even my mouth.

Maynard walks away, and I stand there flanked by flowers and people and putrid perfume. I see my boyfriend, Muddy, out of the corner of my eye, but then things go black. He and the girl he talks to fade away.

In my dream, I am seven years old, playing on the Sit 'N Spin underneath Nina's mahogany dining room table. Nina keeps telling me to stop spinning. "Just stop!"

Thump. The floor reminds me of Lysol and dog pee.

She's right in front of my eyes.

Nina!

We're underneath the colorful Tiffany chandelier in her foyer, and she wears a bumblebee outfit. What the — ? She smiles devilishly and says, "Float like a butterfly, sting like a razor cut. Run as fast and far as you can toward The FINISHED LINE." Then she floats in the air, buzzing, buzzing, buzzing. She reads CosmoGIRL! *magazine.*

I totally know what everything means except for one thing: Nina would never wear a bumblebee suit. I need to hurry up and stop blacking out.

This is Chapter Two.

I am somewhere entirely different the next day, Saturday, but at least I don't see moldy people or smell pink flowers or dream of freaky bumblebees. The walls in the waiting room to the shrink's office are complicated shades of white and cream, like the organza dress in this year's Zac Posen collection, which I *so* cannot spend money on now but might knock off with Nina's awesome Singer Quantum and a roll of pattern paper.

Since she's gone, the sewing machine is mine. All of our sewing supplies, our endless supplies, belong to me.

I look on the positive side. At least the stuff will come in handy when I finally get to New York City to try superhard to win this fashion design contest. Bloomingdale's, my favorite store EVER, created it two years ago for teens in their summer between high school and college. It's called *The Finished Line* (because Nike originally cosponsored it). Now the contest is cosponsored by *CosmoGIRL!,* my favorite magazine ever. (I also live for *Women's Wear Daily* and a blog called www.dressaday.com by a hip seamstress who's obsessed with making fifties dresses from vintage patterns.) I wanted to run off with Nina to New York City next May — "If I'm still alive, darling," she'd say. She told me three times she wouldn't make it past this July. So weird and so sad and so freaking unbelievable. She also said I needed to wait to go to NYC until I definitively earned my diploma *and* gained the capacity to face unpleasantness and frustration, discomfort and defeat, without complaint or collapse.

I'm going to enter that contest, anyway. I am going to the city as fast as I can. I just have to get out of this dreadful place first.

Why does life have to suck so bad sometimes? Crying is weak. Instead, I want to tear apart mass-produced clothing. I want to rip ugly pajamas at the seams. I want to take the caps off bicycle tires. I want to smash Muddy's tiny laptop into a wall and watch the screen shatter, except then I couldn't look online and I'd owe him a new computer, and that would be bad.

Maybe the shrink will help, but I doubt it. See, I'm not freaked out to be here at the Pilgrim Psychiatric Center. I'm instead packed with dread. All my life, if Nina was out hosting a charity event in Saratoga or wherever while Mom traveled to psych wards farther upstate, I'd get dropped off here. When I was little, it was because I needed a babysitter; when I was big, it was to keep me from throwing wild parties. The nurses, Patricia and Cynthia and Viola, are nice, though Patricia moved to New Mexico last year to paint deserts. I usually get my own room, where I am supposed to watch TV, sew, draft, sing, and I'm also allowed to walk on the grounds. I am never supposed to hang out in the lounge with the patients, and I don't. Someone is always in there banging her head on a broomstick or, much worse, moaning. All this is sort of normal to me. Some kids get a nanny or day care; my mom got free sitting at the psych ward.

I've been here since last night, but I'm peeved because the place is booked, and I didn't get my own room. I'm going to complain about it to the shrink; I hope it's one of the shrinks I know.

Spin. Spin. Spin.

I chew some superspicy cinnamon Orbit to get it

16

together. I fish around in my backpack for my sunglasses to hide how I feel inside.

Buzz, buzz, buzz.

On the way here last night, my mother said she needed to be alone with her grief, and I needed to be alone with mine. She wouldn't let me stay with Muddy like she thought I had been doing for the five nights since Nina died. He was peeved about that, and they called each other crass body-function names, but I was still groggy. As the world came into focus, they weren't speaking. Muddy held my hand in the backseat when she asked if I was scarred for life from everything that had happened. I let go, leaned forward, and told her I've been scarred since birth because she's my mother. Russ, our driver, asked us to chill and turned up the String Cheese Incident, an awful band because they never seem to sing a chorus.

Mother Heifer didn't need to be alone, by the way. She just wanted to keep me under wraps while she cleared Nina's house. She'll find out soon that nothing much is left. Muddy and I haven't really been at his place for the past five nights. We've been at Nina's, packing from midnight to dawn since she died. Nina left me a note with very specific instructions.

"Next," a male voice calls as he hacks up his esophagus.

His office is white, communal, confining — I use it for inspiration. I create the Incarcerated Barbie Collection on my Hello Kitty sketch pad. I imagine Barbie in a gray-pink horizontal striped jersey shirt-dress sporting a tight military buzz. I scribble her down with the worn-in number two pencil I use for sketching and marking fabric. Barbie wants to look like the other inmates, so they won't pick on her while remaining trendy even under duress.

"You can stop hiding behind your writing utensil," the young therapist says. He turns down the Super Furry Animals music blaring from his computer and burns a candle as if that will hide the smell of ciga-rettes. I've seen *No Fumar* signs all over this joint. I sink into the stiff black leather seat, pencil gripped tight.

"Hi, Dan," I say. He's a friend of my mother's and of Russ's. Double yuck. "Can I have a smoky treat?" I look downward as if I'm talking to the nappy green carpet. I don't smoke, gross; I'm just calling him out.

"You want to get honest?" He blows out the can-dle. "Take off your shades."

"Okay, I won't." Like I'm letting anyone see my red, puffy eyes.

"You're left-handed." He watches me during the long silent pause. "I hear you design and make all of your outfits — the one you have on looks expensive. I know you're emulating Audrey Hepburn. I'm impressed."

"You've got to be kidding me." This guy is a PhD, a total geek, and I bet he's only heard about *Breakfast at Tiffany's* and never really watched it. I do have on my black dress from the funeral yesterday. I'm not ready to take it off even though it could use a dry cleaning.

He leans forward, and his small talk is like begging for something. "Come on, I don't bite," he adds.

"*Eye* do." I'm working on a Southern accent — I've got my reasons. "Can you move your shoulder to the left?" I squint at the white wall. Because I am where I am, I give myself permission to act fruit-filled. It takes me exactly two minutes to do another sketch of Incarcerated Barbie in her striped shirtwaist dress, accessorized with handcuffs and various prison restraints. "I am working on a new collection. What do you think about the name Chicks in Chains?"

He does not move slightly to his left. These shrinks think they are above it all. "Now, [insert my name here] — "

"Let's get one thing straight right now. My name is not something you will ever *ever* say in my presence. *Ever.* If you do" — I start unwrapping the wire end of my spiral sketchbook until I have a one-inch point. The process takes twenty whole seconds, and I cut my knuckle — "I'll poke this wire straight into my jugular."

My mom named me. If I can't get plastic surgery to look less like her, at least I can be called something she didn't choose. I can at least go to New York City as someone new.

"Now, now, we don't need any of that movie-drama monkey business." He leans back, laughs, and puts two hands behind his head.

I'm funny? Shouldn't he be calling security or those nurses with shots that calm people down? Actually, I'm very lucky he doesn't call for backup because that would complicate my escape.

He sits up straight. "We're here to talk about your grandmother."

I'm acting calm as I explode inside. Of course I should discuss her. But it will hurt too much.

"Your mother seems to think you need to vent. She seems to believe you could benefit from opening up emotionally."

"Do you *know* my mother?" I know this is all a setup. "Have you ever seen *her* open up emotionally, like for real?"

"She's a tough gal, that's for sure. All I know is that she is a phenomenal therapist with the abnormal patients, and she's worried about you." Now he's the one looking down at his desk. He knows he shouldn't be seeing me if he knows about me — it's part of some shrink ethical code.

"Please. I bet she doesn't even have to pay for this session." My hands are trembling, making it difficult to draw for a moment. *Get it together.*

"That's enough. So what should I call you, Miss, um — ?" He isn't letting me get to him, which is cold. I yell a foul curse word, the foulest one I know, and he jumps, not daring to utter what I'm called this time. He defends himself immediately. "Okay, I won't say it. You can trust me."

With the moments I have left, I manage to sketch a pantsuit, skirt, tank top, three-piece suit, and a sweater for Barbie's pit bull. The therapist is patient, crossing his legs while he scratches his chin. His desk needs dusting. "It's okay. Silence is nice," he finally says, breaking it. "Let's see, your file states that your grandmother died of an apparent heart attack six days ago, and you were the one who found her lying in her canopy bed. She was wearing, um, some sort of fancy dress."

"*Givenchy*." And it wasn't a heart attack, and she had a four-post bed, not a canopy. But the details are so not his business.

"Yes. I see here that you were drinking, too. An empty bottle of Perrier-Jouët — is that a wine cooler? — was found on the floor."

"It's champagne."

"You arranged for cremation after the funeral service you planned. It was your grandmother's wish that you do these things. Wow. This is heavy for a seventeen-year-old."

"You have no idea what's heavy." I rip out my Incarcerated Barbie sketches and set them on a pile of file folders. He should feel my backpack, for example. I heft mine into the air, and I'm out.

"Don't leave." He stops rubbing his chin and puts his palms on his dirty desk. He follows me into the hall. But he doesn't try very hard because it's not like I'm a paying patient or anything. He only pecks his head outside his office door, not even stepping out to the waiting room. I hear his cell phone ringing. "You're getting a new room, and Viola will be here soon. Your mom wants me to convince you to stay until at least tomorrow."

Of course she does — she thinks that'll give her time to pack and keep Nina's sparkly jewelry, collectible vintage couture and ready-to-wear, the first editions by Vladimir Nabokov and Judy Blume, and, of course, Nina's Folger's cans full of cash. She'll find out soon enough that none of that stuff is left.

23

I run fast through the side-entrance doors because there's no receptionist or security guard there. Like I don't know this place as well as I know math and A-line skirts. I am crazy, yes, but not this kind of crazy. Why couldn't she just send me to summer camp? Or to my dad's for a few days? What a feral pig.

I'm out of here. As I run down the hallway, I reach into my black dress. The note from Nina, written on her Kate Spade vacation stationery, is folded and tucked into my demi-cut bra. I rub it for good luck. (The note, not my bra.)

I run faster. I have all the energy in the world even if I've slept for, like, five minutes in the six days since she died. I rub that note again, and it's the only thing that takes away the empty place and fills it with hope plus one dream.

This is Chapter Three.

Muddy is waiting for me outside of the Pilgrim Psychiatric Center in his 1969 mint-green Thunderbird convertible. His face is pale so I can't enjoy the smooth honey color of his natural year-round tan — and I need to enjoy *something* right now. I want to reach across the shiny black vinyl seats to hug him but there's a chill in the summer air. He does not seem happy about the plan we've concocted. While I was at the psychiatric center, he texted me that he'd mailed twenty boxes to the main New York City post office branch, where we will pick them up when we arrive in about five hours. The Singer Quantum was way too heavy to mail; it's in the trunk.

25

I will think about how our relationship is turning into a portable cooling device *after* we get to our final destination of New York City. We have been together almost two school years, which is longer than three lifetimes when you're love-ADDed like me. Relationships are up and down, and if we're in a slump this week, I'm sure everything will be better next week. We are escaping it all to go to a place where we can forget it all and, hopefully, have it all. There's nothing left for us in the North Country. Definitely nothing for me.

His mouth opens, and I'm sure it's to tell me that everything will be okay; that he's proud of me; that we are brave; that he loves me.

"I'm not taking you to the city," he blurts as he pulls onto the highway.

Either I'm sleep deprived, or I have post-traumatic stress disorder.

"Of course you're not — we're moving there together. We're *both* going. It's a group effort," I say. "I love you so much, Muddy. I can't wait until we have all the time in the world — "

He did not *say what I think he just said, or I am alone.* Forget the time when my ex-best friend Madeleine Baker turned the whole school against me sophomore year because she claimed she saw me doing it in the boiler room with Kenneth Jacobs (re: naughty tattoo artist). I hadn't been — Kenneth-never-Kenny and I were way over by then. I had, however, been in the boiler room with Muddy, who was her boyfriend at the time.

I met Kenneth because he was a guest speaker in

our freshman drawing class. He is rocker-boy hot, and he should be able to kiss better, judging by his looks. He's twenty-one with his own parlor and a reputation for seriously romantic poetry.

What a love rectangle that was. Madeleine made sure I got a scarlet letter for life — she has never been able to take being one-upped by anyone. She made sure Kenneth got banned from giving more presentations at our school, which he didn't deserve. She made sure Muddy suffered, too. It was complicated, as cruel things tend to be.

Muddy and I made it through that. Can't we make it through my Nina's death?

I try the delusional route one more time because I can't take the reality — or his silence. "We'll just go to Montreal instead!" I am faking a great big smile so maybe he won't be able to do this to me. It's the least I can do.

"You can go," he says, knuckles white from how tightly he's holding the worn black leather steering wheel. His hands are all beat up from the canoe he's been making in his basement. "I'm not saying you shouldn't."

"With you, of course." I'm getting it at this moment,

and my throat slides down to my ankles like it did when this whole drama began.

I turn up his Denon stereo — so what if I detest Jane's Addiction? — because I don't want to hear anything more. Maybe if I can't hear, I won't be able to feel. He is on to me and lowers the levels even though it's his favorite song, "Classic Girl."

"Not only are we not going anywhere together, I'm headed to the car wash to scrub all traces of you out of this vehicle. Then you know what I'm doing? I'm going to sleep good for the first time in weeks — *alone* in *my* house. Oh, don't you worry. I will act dumb when your mother comes after me — I know you're better off away from here. The thing is, I am not ready. The world may be big for you, but I don't need all of that." He finds jobs building decks for people in our town who don't pay him fairly because he's just seventeen. He wants to be an engineer and build entire houses, subdivisions even. He can do that anywhere — there are houses and people and backyards from here to Mars. But he always says he wants to do it here in the Adirondacks. "I'm here for you; I'm not abandoning you. I just can't do this right now."

"Hmph." I am explosive. I am deflated.

"It's too intense," he adds as we pass the Saratoga Diner. We're now twenty-five miles away from our hometown, and two-hundred-and-fifty from what was supposed to be our new beginning. "I need space."

"We'll get a two-bedroom!" I feel trapped. The world is closing in on me. *Spin. Buzz.* Instead of exploding, now I'm imploding.

I want to tell Muddy exactly where to stick his steering wheel. I start touching the dashboard with my thumbs and index fingers, leaving traces of me all over it so it will be difficult to clean. I lean across my seat to continue putting my fingerprints on every Thunderbird surface I can reach.

Without actually looking at me, he sees what I'm doing. He speeds up to ninety-seven miles per hour, then hits the brakes and pulls to the shoulder of the road. His head stays facing the highway, steady. If he looks at me, I know he won't be able to do what he's doing. Just six days ago, we were discussing what our kids might look like — tanned with skinny butts. Five days ago, he was crying while we packed Nina's stuff. Four days ago, he didn't say much. But after that, I only remember different shades of blur.

"I need you!" I say, and I really, really, really do. I am,

for all practical purposes, mad about him even when I do hate him. There were two people in this world I had to love. One of them left me forever, and the other is now releasing himself from responsibility. My skin might as well come off. I imagine being alone, so alone, that no one will check on me when I go to bed at night or wake in the morning. Without Nina and now Muddy, no one will even know if I get hit by a taxicab. No one will care.

I can't do this.

I don't want to do this.

I will do this.

I think with my heart, and I say with my mouth, "A seventeen-year-old girl can't exactly go to New York City by herself — even if her wardrobe is well thought out."

"The whole world doesn't revolve around your latest Breakfast dress pattern or invisible zipper!" He is shaking his head back and forth, his dark curly hair flopping around angrily.

"And I'm sick of hearing about your circular saw." I actually love hearing about his circular saw. I love seeing his designs. I hate him, though, right now. More than he knows.

"See, you don't need me. The only person you've ever needed is yourself," he says, and I think he's getting a little upset — about what, I don't know. His boyfriend isn't breaking up with him; he's not the one being apprehended by Hogzilla and the local psychiatric ward; his grandmother, the only person he could truly count on in the world, didn't just kick the bucket in a four-post bed in front of his face.

I mutter angry things at him. Then I yell them. It's not pretty. *Get it together,* I scream in my head to myself. I hate losing control.

I curl my fists into balls and hit his thighs. I hit and hit and hit, but he sits calmly looking at the trees far away, over the top of my head.

"You're done now." He looks at my hands, grabs them, and restrains them. He is way emotionless, and that's because he's got a button for his feelings, and it's switched to off.

"My hands hurt." I am not crying. I am absolutely *not* crying.

"We decided we are antiviolence, remember? Now if you can sit still long enough, I'll drop you at the bus station in Albany. But that's as far as you and me are going." We are still on the shoulder of the road. He drops my hands and looks over his left shoulder at the traffic.

"You'll miss me," I say, tightening my two ponytails before they wiggle free. I dyed my blond hair jet-black ten days ago. Nina dug it. Muddy not so much.

"Maybe. But I won't miss the constant drama. I won't miss the schemes. I won't miss the way you put your feet up on the dashboard of my car. I won't miss the way you leave magazines all over my floor. I won't miss the smell of your nail polish. I won't miss having to follow your schedules and your to-do lists. I won't miss the nasty phone calls from your deranged, psychotic mother. I won't miss the black combat boots and heels you leave in the kitchen for me to trip on. I won't miss the way you always change my computer's home page. I won't miss accidentally sitting down on a bunch of straight pins that shouldn't be anywhere near the couch. And, most of all, I won't have to clean up your messes ever again."

"But how could you leave me at a time like this?" I'm sitting still now, and I'm so glad I kept my sunglasses on. "Does this have to do with Madeleine?"

"You know I don't talk to her." He is looking at me dead on — too dead on, if you ask me.

"I saw you talk to her yesterday, when I blacked out." I am getting a clear flash of it now. They smiled at each other from the farthest side of the room by all those flowers. She batted her eyes at him, and then she looked at me. They got closer; they talked. That's when I went down.

"When you black out, you can't see anyone." Now he's concentrating on his ignition and considering going way too fast again. But he pulls the key out and sets it in his lap. I think I believe him. He adds, "This isn't the end I wanted. Don't think this is easy for me. In fact, just *don't think*." His voice crackles when he says this.

"Am I supposed to feel sorry for *you*? Go find a tree — there's one over there — and climb it." I'm checking his eyes for signs of anything. "Since you love trees and mountains and this stupid North Country so freaking much."

When Madeleine dumped and branded me, Muddy became my best friend. He and I have been through it all. He got suspended from school. His parents threw him out, Nina took him in, then he moved back home. We both had our issues in the last two years. But it was okay because we had each other.

Now he keeps going with his low baritone voice, and I tune him out so he can't hurt me any more than he already has. My heart is still stuck down in my ankles, but I'm trying to mentally pull it back up and pull myself together.

I've got a Greyhound to catch.

I've got a city to live in.

I've got a contest to enter.

I've got a department store to visit where every-thing will be fine, just fine.

Heartbreak of all kinds has to go on the bottom of my to-do list for now. Getting out of town is tops, especially now.

"I know one thing you'll really miss," I huff, kicking his glove box open and taking something out. His foot presses the gas pedal while his hand slams it shut.

"Yeah, whatever you've gotten out of my glove box," he says, but he doesn't tell me to put it back. The rims of his eyes are scary red.

"Do you still care about me?"

He speeds up. Faster. Faster. Faster. He doesn't answer. He is looking at the road, but I'm sure he doesn't see it. The car's speed is a rush for both of us — but not the good kind.

The wind is loud, so I yell. "This sux." I won't take it. "This is a pathetic end to us. At least let's end this stylishly. Pull over, and I'll hitch a ride."

He swerves the Thunderbird to the shoulder of Interstate 87 South, reaches across me and brushes my chest as he opens the passenger door.

We do not hug. We do not kiss. We stare each other down in a face-off that lasts forty-three seconds, and I am counting. I can barely keep myself together, but I win. After looking away, he is gone.

I fish around in my backpack, find my cell phone, and throw it as hard as I can in the direction of the Thunderbird. A jacked-up truck promptly smashes it into four thousand bytes.

There, the temptation is gone.

Losing my mobile device is like having knives slice through my gloves and skin. But it hurts in a good way. Without a cell, he can't reach me, and I can't text him. No one can reach me: not Madeleine or Trina or Sally or Lexi with the pranks, not Kenneth with the texts, not Hogzilla with the threats, not Muddy with

35

whatever. But part of the reason I threw it was because, deep down, I know Muddy won't call or text at all. When he makes a decision, the decision is made.

So, like him, I'm making my own decision this nanosecond:

If I'm going to be on my own, I'm going to be on my own.

I've always wanted to do this, to go to New York City and follow my dreams. So what if I have to do it alone.

My next mental list:

1. Heart demolished? Check.

2. Backpack in hand? Check.

3. Ponytails tight? Check.

4. Stash of money from Muddy's glove box in pocket? Check.

The least that deserter can do is pay for a girl's bus ticket. I wonder if they have Greyhound First Class?

I tell myself to stay positive, *it could be worse.* But honestly, it couldn't. I'm standing there about to do the one thing I absolutely cannot tolerate. The water behind my eyes gains force. I tell those tears to dry the mother-H up. *Just dry up. Just. Dry. Up.* They don't want to, but they do.

I can't stand on the side of Interstate 87 looking like a fugitive or appearing vulnerable. I stand up straighter than I've ever stood in my life. I put on my Tutti Fruiti Lancôme lip gloss. I pull down my short black shift. I point my toe — a vintage Mary Jane with a satin black strap and mother-of-pearl ankle button I added myself — in the direction of the heavy traffic. I flash a tad of leg. I hope for a safe ride.

Muddy's gone and so are the almost-tears. I get the feeling I'm going to be okay.

Hogzilla institutionalized me.

Muddy abandoned me.

Nina had a fake heart attack and a real death.

But I am here.

I know I'm here because the cut on my middle knuckle is totally starting to bleed. The pain is exquisite proof that I have made it through what I thought I couldn't. The wind blows past my face like life blows by when you're sitting in your small upstate New York hometown spinning, spinning, and spinning.

I'll put my thumb up — as soon as I put on Nina's black satin gloves.

This is Chapter Four.

I've been out here ten minutes and nada.

I think how Nina was going to help me get an apartment in New York City after I graduated. She'd heard about my dream — our dream — at least three times a day for the last two years. We would become a respected design team: She sewed better than I did; I had more ideas than she did. She was calm and self-assured; I was hyper and self-conscious. We get — I mean *got* — along great even when we disagreed. We didn't have to be famous; we just wanted to see our clothes in Bloomingdale's. There weren't any famous grandmother-granddaughter designer teams, so we were going to be the first. Our line was going to be called Breakfast . . . so we'd have Breakfast at Bloomingdale's every single day.

That's what I believed. I have to believe, or I have nothing else.

Nina and I must have watched the movie *Breakfast at Tiffany's* at least two hundred times, and the clothes in it are enough to make a girl get up in the morning. We loved giving classy sixties-style clothes lighthearted hipster, goth, and rocker-girl twists. Holly Golightly, the movie's main character, was our muse. We'd often ask each other, "What would Holly wear?"

My strongest designs are based on one idea: What would Holly Golightly be into if she were seventeen years old today? Lots of people have been inspired by Audrey, sure, but not as many by Holly Golightly in particular. Audrey's class was the sure thing because she grew up in Europe, overcame extreme hardship in World War II, took serious ballet classes, spoke lots of languages, and was the daughter of a real baroness. Holly, on the other glove, was newfound culture, even counterculture in her time. She came from a crappy town; she wanted to improve her status at any cost; she had confidence; she believed what she believed no matter what; she got her way; she hid her sadness behind a tough exterior; she hung out with guys; she was tiny yet larger than any one person's life.

I'm inspired by the idea that every girl is a little Holly. Every guy wants a girl who is a little Holly. Holly Golightly is more than a fictional character to me.

Now I truly feel like I am channeling Holly. She lost the only person in the world she loved, too.

My mind goes back to six months ago: "Do you

like this short inseam?" Nina was holding up a black leather skirt — think Madonna and a roller-skating rink. She had just watched *Garden State* (it took her a while sometimes), so she was into the Shins. This happy, dippy music was playing, songs like "Know Your Onion." Nina took off her small, oval tortoise-shell glasses to inspect the skirt closer because she refused to get bifocals. I remember hoping my hair would look thick and blond like hers when I turned seventy-one. I hoped my dye job would be just as good. She would pull the bangs back with a barrette that matched her glasses. She was taller and leaner than me, with the posture of a young ballerina in her trademark black four-inch heels. She always had her look together, even when she went to bed. Her Betsey Johnson nightclothes matched. Her daytime ward-robe — over the years, she'd collected fifties Givenchy, sixties Chanel, seventies Pucci — looked like a maga-zine's fashion closet. My Nina never went out of the house without a killer label. Labels don't excite me as much, but designs, fabric, colors, and moods do. I couldn't fork over cash I didn't have for the real deals, so Nina helped me make look-alikes that surpassed the originals.

"Too short," I said, admiring her because she was my Nina and barely looking at the skirt. They were always showing unmentionables, and I'd have to tell her to make them longer. "A Holly could only wear that skirt if she had on her best pair of Hanky Pankies and she meant for the whole world to see them." That's what we called my future customers: Hollys.

"You young people . . ." She was huffing even though she usually had to make a racy and then a real version of just about every outfit she dreamed up. ". . . Always wanting to cover yourselves up. You should show it while you have it."

"When have you not had it?" I said, nose back down to the Singer Quantum so I could sew on the curve without putting another needle through my left pointer finger.

41

I know Nina would've loved this Miss Golightly dress I made for her funeral. I feel I cannot take it off until I reach my destination . . . so I'd better reach New York soon before I start to smell.

I put my thumb back up where it was, the perfect ninety-degree angle covered in black satin.

I fake my sweetest smile.

No more thinking is allowed. Not now.

A green and stainless steel Zap Trucks semi pulls over, with a woman at the wheel. The side of the truck has a logo in quotes: "NEED IT FAST? COUNT ON ZAP!" The driver looks like she can bench-press a brick oven. Her hair is tied back in a red bandanna. Trucker stylish. I can picture her on Nina's Tiffany-blue 1968 Vespa VLB Sprint.

"I'm Betsy." She is checking her teeth in her rearview mirror. "Get in."

She offers to take me to Rochester, but I'm pretty sure they don't have a Bloomingdale's there. Luckily, she doesn't mind dropping me off at the Albany bus terminal on Hamilton Street, where the Greyhound picks up wishful New York City–bound passengers.

"You have to be more careful," she says, and I think Nina would have dug her. "What's your name, little gal?"

My heart revs up. I don't want her to know. I don't want to make her an accomplice. "It's Destinee," I lie.

"Rule Number One, and I get the feeling you're new at running away, don't ever tell no one your name." She gives me a card — truckers have business cards? — and pointers for hopping on freight trains without getting any limbs cut off. Apparently, the best place to catch one is in Rensselaer County.

"Gotcha," I say. She winks, and I think she gets me. A few minutes rumble by in the passenger's side of the semi while she sings Bon Jovi's "Blaze of Glory."

"Mother shucks!" I yell.

Betsy is so frazzled that her bandanna falls off. She fishes around for it while she's trying to drive, which scares me. "What, did I hit a bunny again? Oh, man, I hate when that happens."

"No, no, the super furry animals are safe."

"Why scare me, then!" This wasn't a question. She shoves her bandanna back into place. "Blaze of Glory" ends.

"Sorry, I just, um, forgot to feed my turtle," I say, lying again. The real reason I'm over the edge: My Singer Quantum sewing machine is still in the back of the Thunderbird.

This sucks.

This is Chapter Five.

This guy next to me, the one whose right arm is creeping way too close to my thigh, is slobbering. I can smell it. It reeks like beer mixed with chocolate. This is such a shame because a) judging by his Shins (he actually knows who they are!) T-shirt, he's my age, and b) he could be cute if he'd just take off the trucker hat and shave the fuzz above his lips.

He looks a little like Muddy, who, understandably, I need revenge on.

I flirt.

"You ride the Greyhound bus, like, a lot?"

"Only when I can sit next to girls like you," he says, pulling one earbud out of his right ear. "Have you ever done any performing?"

"Why, yes. I dance topless Tuesdays at Spanks in Times Square." I am just trying to entertain myself. It can't hurt.

"Wow! Me, too!" His face is in the shape of an exaggerated O. "But this is my first time on the bus. The flight I needed got canceled and my dad flushed my car keys down the toilet — well, they wouldn't flush, so he had to stick the bowl scrubber down there and force them. Whatever — the keys are in the Hudson by now."

"I'm actually a bus virgin, too." I am trying out a proper fake English accent, the kind actresses used in movies from the dark ages. I thought I'd see if that worked better than the Southern belle drawl.

"With the accent, and that sleeping pillow thing, I guessed you were a world traveler." He fiddles with his music player, increasing the blare of the Misfits. The coincidences are weird. I know this punk band, an original and ancient one (from the eighties!), because Nina was into that scene way back when. The Misfits were into Marilyn Monroe like Nina and I were into Audrey/Holly. I even know the song this dude is blasting. It's an early one called "Teenagers from Mars."

We want, we need it, we'll take it
We want, we need it, we'll take it, baby

I can't help but mouth the lyrics. That's when he turns toward me, really toward me, his back facing the center aisle of the bus. I check out his footwear — I have the hots for illicit bowling shoes, the kind you get at the bowling alley by walking out without retrieving the shoes you came in with. But those things don't matter; his backpack does.

"I tire rather easily." I blow air into the sleeping doughnut I bought in Albany with seven dollars of Muddy's money. I'll leave it on the seat after the ride — maybe it'll help the next weary traveler. "Actually, I was quite wondering if I could lean on your backpack for a catnap. I mean, if there's nothing in there you need terribly."

"You want my backpack?" He smirks the way that guys do when they're trying to bargain for something.

"I don't want *it*. I just want to lean on it," I say, flipping on my brat switch. My posture becomes straightened and I cock my head to one side while I roll my eyes.

His eyes sort of cross. Either he is mentally challenged, which I doubt, or as tired as I am, or drunk. "Yeah, like, okay," he says.

Score. You can't have what you don't ask for. I've found that face-to-face requests rarely get answered no.

As he hands me the bag, which I prop between

myself and the window, I pull out my own music player, blare a song called "Damn It Feels Good to Be a Gangsta," and pretend to nap. He watches me for a while, like he expects me to provide brilliant conversation or keep him cozy. Then, one hour later, he does exactly what I want. He falls asleep.

I can't help it. I reach into my backpack and slip a green Tic Tac into his piehole.

Much better.

Plus, my stomach is now filled with the king-size bag of Almond M&M's that were tucked just inside his backpack. I had seen him eating them before we boarded. I found a bonus bag of sour-cream-and-onion chips. They were unopened until I opened them. I left his two cans of Pabst Blue Ribbon alone. Yuck. I prefer Perrier-Jouët but only on special occasions like D-day, breakups, breakthroughs, and Groundhog Day.

He is stirring. *Uh-oh.* He will see that his backpack has been safely placed by his feet, exactly where it was before I made my request. I do not feel like conversation. I am feeling my food coma.

He gets up to use the bus bathroom, taking his backpack with him. Upon return, he asks me, "Hey, by any chance, did you eat my chips?"

47

"Are you kidding? I hate chips," I say, pretending I'm busy fishing around in my own bag. I pull out a *National Enquirer* that I borrowed from the Pilgrim Psychiatric Center waiting room.

"Wait a minute, where's your fake English accent?" he says, his brows melding together. He's got thick eyelashes for a guy.

"I mean, I quite hate chips," I say with the verbal inflections that aren't going to make anyone believe that I'm British. I decide to try Southern belle once again later. I can make it work.

"I don't buy it for a second. Hey, and what about my M&M's?" He looks really peeved.

I look more peeved. I turn my magazine to the page about badly dressed celebrities as I turn the volume up.

Damn it feels good to be a gangsta.

Part 2
THEN THERE'S A FRESH START
IN THE CITY.

This is Chapter Six.

Trucker Hat is not speaking to me. He huffs to the back of the moving vehicle.

Thank goodness for food and silence.

Our ghetto wagon crosses the Hudson River. We are about to arrive at the Port Authority bus terminal, the one that's on Forty-Second Street and Eighth Avenue, according to my *Time Out New York* guidebook. The guy at the ticket counter had also explained this to me before we left. He said I'd be one block (how far can a block be?) from Times Square. Of course, right before we boarded this traffic-puppy, he also told me the ladies' room was closed and pointed me toward the men's. When I walked in — to see guys standing at urinals (ick) — he yelled that he was kidding, and I had better be less gullible or I'll get sold into prostitution in New York City. I relieved myself in the ladies' room — even though it *was* closed, thankyouverymuch — then asked to borrow the ticket guy's pen. I threw it in the trash can right in front of his face. Why did I do that? I still feel kind of bad, but I'm not having the best of weekends.

50

Trucker Hat saw that exchange (and the toilet paper clinging to my shoe). And so did the toothless man sitting behind me. So did the woman one row ahead who bought two tickets (one for her, one for her butt). So did the four little old ladies who are also on this ghetto wagon somewhere. And so did the guy/girl combo who sit in the back looking like they just inhaled E or bus fumes. They all thought it was funny, but I wasn't sure if the joke was on me or the ticket guy or on the random coincidences of the universe.

I think the joke was on me.

Immediately upon my arrival in the Big Apple — I hope the city is a green apple because red is too sweet — everything's going to be different. In a big, crowded, wide-awake place, you can remake yourself. It's where you go if you want to move with the crowd, but in a way that stands out. It's where you go if you know you're different from the people around you, but you're not sure if that's good or bad.

In New York, watch me be anything. Or nothing. Or something.

I'm not scared of the big city. As long as I don't see homeless people, drug addicts, armed policemen, or pigeons, I will be fine. I'll never open my wallet and count my money in public — that will be easy, considering I don't believe in wallets. And I have told myself over and over that I will not make eye contact with anyone, unless he's around my age and as delicious as a king-size bag of red M&M's.

I'm honestly a whole lot more scared of Hogzilla finding me than I am of anything else. She's flipping right this second — I know it as well as I know my name — because Nina's house has been cleaned out. But that's nothing compared to what she'll do when she finds out the money is not hers but mine. I did talk Nina into leaving Hogzilla the million-dollar Victorian house, but I have a feeling my mother won't be appreciative. She doesn't care about nesting. I can't think of any other reason she'd come looking for me. Unless she wants to try to find a way to get me locked up — like in maximum-security federal natural-born-killer prison — for finding my dead grandmother and waiting several hours before calling the police. Is that a crime? What about borrowing someone's M&M's?

I turn eighteen in December, and then the money is mine as long as I have my high school diploma: Nina's rules are to keep me in a perfect straight-stitch line. This stupid diploma is kinking up everything as something always does. I just have to stay away from upstate this summer and fall and, like, the rest of my life. All I need is food and shelter and fashion, not in that order. I wonder where Trucker Hat lives in the city, but I figure I shouldn't have chowed on his food if I'd wanted to make friends and freeload.

I wouldn't have been able to be friends with him, anyway. He looks a little too much like the boy in the Thunderbird.

I put my sunglasses back on superfast. I turn up my Geto Boys song, and I am able to force myself to relax. *Come on. Just. Relax.*

It takes several deep breaths. I'm almost fine or close enough. I close my eyes and dream of Bloomingdale's — its big brown bags, its well-made clothes that make imperfect people look perfect — until the bus driver flips his top. Whenever I'm freaking from now on, I will think of Bloomingdale's.

He yells, "Hey, kid, get the hell off this bus. No way are you making me late for my back wax!"

I lay there a second on the pillow I will leave behind. For this moment, I feel calmer than I've felt in six hours, six days, six months. I want to remember what it feels like to be fine or close enough.

This is Chapter Seven.

I am my own problem now. No rules for me, not ever. I am not one to brag or anything, but I've got an unusually high maturity level.

Everything will be okay, will make sense, if I just get to Bloomingdale's.

I have some pesky logistics to figure out once I get there. I plan to sit down in a dressing room and make a list. Like, how do I get anywhere in this city? I can't even find my way around the Port Authority. Nina brought me to the city to see the tents in Bryant Park during Fashion Week when I was six and again when I was twelve. We went to Serendipity for iced hot chocolate and the MoMA for Andy Warhol. What I really remember is the blue-cheese-feet odor of the taxicabs. We kept meaning to come back but there was always so much to do — like attend my mother's latest wedding or watch movies or sneak away to Maine for much-needed, serene sewing vacations by the beach. We didn't make enough time to go back to New York City because I always thought we'd live here for good when I graduated. I dreamed of attending the Fashion Institute of Technology, the coolest fashion school not only because it was New York City's first, but also because Calvin Klein, Carolina Herrera, Michael Kors, and Michelle Smith (Milly is my absolute to-die-for favorite!!!) went there. Nina said I wouldn't even have to live in the dorm — I'd get a huge apartment like the ones you see on *Friends* reruns and MTV. I dreamed of becoming a budding-fashion-designer/salesgirl at Bloomingdale's — I'd even settle for Saks. Well, maybe.

Nothing looks familiar or like how I imagined New York City would look. Where are the expensive shoes? The MTV studios? The reporters with cameras and notebooks? The foulmouthed deli guys and the pizza? Maybe Nina was right, and I should've waited till I graduated. But more time with Hogzilla without Nina? I'd turn into a daughter-sicle on an Adirondack mountaintop.

I kind of start freaking, so I start writing by numbers.

1. Shelter.

2. Food.

3. Fashion.

Yes, I've covered that. What else is there?

4. Just friends and friends with benefits. I definitely need benefits.

Oh, yeah, money.

5. Money.

Whatever cash I do have, I can thank Madeleine for it. Before she excommunicated me at the start of sophomore year, I made clothes for all the girls in our class from geek to cheerleader captain (aka Madeleine) in exchange for them being my fashion guinea pigs. I've been trying to make the transition from seamstress to fashion designer — not easy — for years now. Nina financed me, calling this the most important part of my education. But after the Kenneth/me/boiler room lie, Madeleine made sure no one — not even our old friends Trina and Sally and Lexi — would wear my new Breakfast-brand skirts and dresses. Even if they wanted to, they didn't because they never knew if they would be in her roasting pan next.

Only Muddy would talk to me, because he'd been excommunicated, too, for choosing me over her. Not only for macking me but also for a different reason that got him expelled from school. He isn't into football because he thinks it's barbaric/homoerotic, the way guys beat one another down and then pat butts. He believes men should only be barbaric when necessary. And according to him, necessity was everywhere at the beginning of our sophomore year. He beat down Kenneth minus the pat on the butt, only because he thought Kenneth had been inappropriate with me.

With Madeleine out of my life, I had time. Since kindergarten, she'd kept me busy dyeing her hair, letting out her shirts to accommodate her boobs (she got them at age eight), making lists of who was in and out at school, and reading about boy dramas via IM and texts until one A.M. I swore I would be bored and empty without the girlie high school activities I was used to. But I wasn't. I had been more bored and more empty when I was popular.

Unpopular, I was just empty.

I withdrew from whatever social scene Queensbury High has, and I started doing alterations for a local boutique called Miss Priss, which let me sell a few of my designs, too. In between doing that job, taking online calculus to get it over with, and hanging out with my shiny new boyfriend, Muddy *(spit on floor and rub in with Mary Jane)*, I was too busy to notice when people started noticing me again at the beginning of junior year.

Madeleine, of course, stayed popular. Our friends took her side, as I'd always been her funky, weird, background best friend. I was the one, in middle school, who carried the Cokes as we pranced past boys at the pool. I was the one who brought the iPod and deejayed the parties while she danced. Madeleine tells great jokes and then tells you off. People, me included, live for abuse. People, me included, love beauty, too, as if it will rub off. Hot people like Madeleine always have it easier. (I'm okay looking and not totally fug, but I'm not hot like her.)

I didn't have friends besides Muddy. The more alone I was, the cooler I became. People forgot the dirty rumors eventually. But they still watched me. I pretended to be over everything — earbuds from music player inserted at all times, cell phone glued to left side of face during lunch and free period, sketchbook opened during all school activities. I heard whispers like "Who is she really? What do you think she's listening to? What are the adults-only parties at her Nina's like? Maybe she could get us invited?"

It wasn't the same kind of cool I'd been when Madeleine and I were best friends. We had been totally predictable in that Hollywood blockbuster way. Alone, I became more like an independent movie that didn't make any sense but was worth watching, anyway. By the end of the year, I had some sort of messed-up, underground credibility at Queens-bury High. Muddy, who had immersed himself in his after-school jobs and us, saw the same thing happen. We were the town's mysterious couple.

The point is, thanks to Madeleine or the lack of Madeleine, I had more time to work and saved Miss Priss money, one thousand two hundred fifty-five dollars and twenty-three cents, in a bank account. Plus, I have all the money I found in the Folger's cans throughout Nina's grand Victorian house, and that is another three thousand one hundred sixty-seven dollars and twenty-five cents. I am going to do what Nina told me to do with it. (I rub the note she wrote in my bra for dramatic effect.) I'm using it wisely.

Meanwhile, I have access to her personal bank account until whatever trust fund she created for me kicks in. That is money I will use conservatively and only when I have to, pre- and post-trust fund. I will not blow it on Birkin bags or Manolo shoes like she did, and especially not on extravagant parties that I'd have to DJ. She told me to always live like I didn't have money if I wanted to be happy.

I wander into the restaurant that looks the cleanest, called Au Bon Pain, a name I don't dare try to pronounce. A combo meal is two hundred dollars — well, it's eight-fifty. That seems like a lot to spend on lunch, but all the dirtier restaurants cost this much or more. All I know is that I'm about to die — M&M's and chips on the bus weren't enough — so I order a grilled chicken Caesar salad and a banana. I don't even get an iced cappuccino because I want to practice spending carefully. I am paranoid that I will run out of cash. My mind races in lists:

1. Spend no more than eight dollars on each meal.

2. Spend no more than seventy-five dollars a day to make cash last as long as possible, and get a job.

3. Spend as little as humanly possible on rent or find a sympathetic person to provide.

4. Win contest, start climbing fashion ladder, be respected for skills and provide for self.

5. Never rely on Nina's money because:

a) Hogzilla will do anything — *everything* — to

keep it for herself; h) Nina's money didn't equal happiness for her, as she liked to remind me. But success did, and that's what I want.

6. Forget high school, get GED ASAP — and go to college, ugh sigh, only if I don't end up with a real fashion job somewhere. I don't believe in Plan Bs because then people get lazy and don't make Plan A work. So that's *not* Plan B.

I've always used Nina's checking account for expenses, like for shampoo and multivitamins and Mondo Mango drinks from TCBY. My mom never gave me a dime — three-times-divorced shrinks don't have many dimes, anyway. In fact, she sponged off Nina, too, but I stayed out of their arrangement. They must've had an arrangement or Hogzilla wouldn't have been able to drive a Volvo. Nina was cool about supporting me within reason, thankfully. The time Muddy and I road-tripped and stayed at Le St-James in Montreal, though? Nina said that was not reasonable. I had to pay her back, which meant adding extra hours at Priss. She advised me on how to spend. Her rules were easy: 1) never too much, and 2) must be marked down at least once. I wonder how that's going to work now that she's dead. I have to make my own calls now, which is about as safe as standing in front of a hot garment steamer.

The reality is that her account, my current lifeline, could dry up no matter how fat it is and how careful I am. Since I am a fugitive and a runaway and maybe even wanted, my mother could have that account blocked at any time, couldn't she? Or maybe the bank will find out that she's no longer alive and kill the funds. Or maybe they'll see where I make withdrawals and find me. *Oh, God, no. Oh, no.* Or worse, maybe just maybe someone will steal my card and use it to buy out Target. Do they have Target in this city? I hope so — wait — maybe I don't.

It's hard to think because from what I can tell so far, New York gets into your head. My ears ring from the silent loud sounds of busy-ness — restaurants frying food, people asking for spare change, pedestrians bustling, cars banging, taxis honking, and slicksters handing me flyers that I immediately throw in the trash. My eyes are overloaded with the brown of this building, the colors of all the people, the selection of magazines, the corridors all leading to somewhere different. Through the blindness of sensory surplus, I see a Bank of America ATM. I push the PIN numbers,

1212. That is my birthday. Out pops the daily limit on Nina's account, five hundred dollars, all in twenties. I see a fat balance left on the receipt.

Wow.

And there's more in the trust fund with my name on it. I know there's a lot, but I don't know how much. If money were fabric, I'd understand it. But it's not.

I think about the Singer Quantum, how I'd love to be on it, doing a perfectly tidy zipper into my favorite sixties gathered skirt that looks hot with crinoline under it. I think about the shirtwaist dresses made with vintage fabric that I totally die for. I fill my mind with designs — shift dresses and skinny black pants and muted color palettes — so I'll stop freaking. I can't think of anything worse than fainting on this sticky Au Bon Pain floor.

Get it together. Get. It. Together.

As long as I'm working hard toward *the goal, our goal* — Breakfast at Bloomingdale's — I'm not going to feel guilty about living off her bank account. But that's not what I really feel unsure about. I feel far more doubtful about taking off for New York before she wanted me to.

I try to be positive as I head out of Au Bon Pain.

Yes, Holly Golightly would be positive. After all, there's no joy in knowing the outcome of one's journey.

I see Trucker Hat buy a hot dog from a vendor who just spent three whole seconds scratching way down in his shoe, pulling up a dingy sock, and scraping between his big and second toes. I walk up behind TH and wish I had been nicer on the Smellhound. He's the only person I kind-of-sort-of know in New York City.

And he hates me.

"You." He waves his hot dog at me.

"Me." I am, at this moment, wondering what he sees. Do I look hot or silly in my black shift on a Sunday afternoon? Does it look like I've been wearing the same outfit for two days? Does my superstuffed backpack make me look like a tourist? Are my ponytails all lopsided *again*? Why am I standing here questioning myself?

"That guy you bought that hot dog from — " I began to tell him.

"What, you want this, too? Here." He hands the half-eaten hot dog to me in a way that if I don't take it, it's going to be all over my dress. I hold the wiener, and I get the urge to wash my hands.

"No, thanks." I just play along. I stand up straight; I look okay. He looks okay, too. Like he's washed his face, rinsed out his mouth, and stopped buzzing from the Pabst Blue Ribbon plus chocolate.

I look inside the white shopping bag he's holding from the huge drugstore I just passed called Duane Reade. (How do I pronounce that?) I scan what he bought: Q-Tips, shaving cream, foot powder, soap, toothbrush, Crest, and Cracker Jacks. He reaches into his bag and holds out Orbit gum. "Definitely take this. You have garlic breath."

Darn that potent Caesar salad! He stands close to me. I feel excited first. I feel devastated second. The last time I was close, I was with Muddy, assaulting him during our breakup while he just sat there.

I throw out the hot dog, and luckily he doesn't say anything more about it.

Chewing spicy cinnamon loudly and snapping it for brat effect, I say, "So, I apologize about the M&M's. Can I owe you some?"

"If you owe me, does that mean I have to see you again? Let me think a minute . . . no." He chews a piece of gum, too.

"Are you from here?" I'm speaking carefully, slowly.

65

No English accent. I'm working my Georgia peach again.

"Are you?" He is scanning the people around us. I wonder what he's looking for. His gaze stops on me.

"I'm not," I say.

"I can tell." Now he is scanning my dress, my backpack, my hair. I am not even one bit nervous.

Hmph. "How?" I'm fiddling with my fingernails. I'm not nervous at all. My black heels hurt.

"You clearly don't know your way around the Port Authority. After you got off the bus, you went left — and left is toward the bus that goes to IKEA. Then you went in a circle to find a restaurant that was right in front of you. Then you went the long way to an ATM." His arms move around a lot when he talks. He's passionate.

"Creepy. You're following me."

"I wasn't, actually. I had to check the times for the IKEA bus, then I went into Au Bon Pain for a large mocha cappuccino. Then I went into Duane Reade, and when I came back, you were still walking around out here. I was hoping you would've found your way out to Eighth Avenue before I finished this hot dog, though. That so obviously didn't happen." I like the way he leans in when he talks. Also, I learn that you pronounce Au Bon Pain like "Ahh Bon Pan" and Duane Reade like "Dwayne Reed."

"I'm lost. Maybe you could show me?" I just want him to stay for a second. I'm sick of talking to myself.

"Okay. Turn around," he says, stepping back so he can point in that direction. "And go up those stairs to Gate One-fifty-five."

"That's the bus back to Albany."

"It goes all the way to Montreal, if you want to know the truth. Take it." He's not standing near me anymore; he's heading out the door.

I run in front of him and plant myself. He could easily go around me, but he doesn't. I ask, "Listen, can I just say I'm sorry and then ask you a favor?"

67

"Sure."

"My crack-addict grandfather burned his own house down in Albany, and it's a long story, but we didn't have any place to live after that. And so he took some more crack, and that made him crazy, so he threw me out. For no reason! So I'm here. I'm alone. I have nothing but the clothes in my backpack and a truckload of boxes waiting for me at the post office. I'm starting over. Here. In New York." I'm trying to make this sound important, but it's coming out laughable. He's laughing.

"That sucks. Good luck." He goes around me, walking toward the big exit doors. "You have no idea what I just went through — and I'm not even making up stories like you are. Anyway, you expect me to believe that girls with crack-addict grandfathers wear black satin gloves? What do you take me for? A clown?"

"Wait! I'll tell the truth: I haven't been to the city since I turned six, or wait, I think I was twelve. It's just that I truly don't know where to go." At the realization that I sound desperate, I trail behind him but stop following. I'm just headed out, too.

"Buy a book." He flails his arms up over his head. Then he reaches in his bag for the Cracker Jacks. I don't say I already have a guidebook; that would defeat my purpose

"Okay, I get it." We're now outside. He turns left. I turn right. I yell, "Have a just-okay life!"

I have never seen so many taxicabs in my life. They are yellow, and they line up in front of the Port Authority. All four thousand and fifty of them are honking. Two million people holding suitcases throw their hands in the air so one of the cars will choose them. I look up and expect to see the sky. All I see are lights and concrete. I grab my backpack tighter because there are a whole lot of people touching me, not on purpose, but because the sidewalk is densely populated.

I'm alone.

I'm alone.

And I thought I was alone before.

I decide to stand my ground. I have to wait a second until I know where to go. I have to wait a second because this truly is my first impression of my new home, and I want to remember it. Flashes like lightning flicker through my head — flashes of businesspeople and immigrants and Disney shows on Broadway and billboards for Red Stripe. The smell of garbage mixed with roasting nuts tingles my nostrils. I'm scared but not scared.

I'm breathing.

I'm breathing.

I can't breathe.

"Get the eff off me," I'm yelling as someone tugs my backpack from behind. Note to self: Holly would never say eff. She wouldn't even think it. I must revise myself.

It's Trucker Hat. "You also owe me a bag of sour-cream-and-onion chips."

I have an urge to apologize. I don't, though. *What's my problem?*

The staring match between us begins, and we both ask the same question at once. "What do you want?"

This is Chapter Eight.

Trucker Hat and I share a moment, share some info, and then he goes his way and I move to find mine. Soon enough, I'm back inside the Port Authority, navigating my way down an escalator where the subway is supposed to be. *Stop bruising me.* An elderly Asian wacks me to the right side of the moving staircase with his cane so he can pass on the left. He's a D, cane or no cane. I didn't know Manhattan would be so physical.

"I need to go to Bloomingdale's," I say when it is finally my turn to buy something called a Metrocard that will pay for my ride.

"Don't we all?" asks the subway employee through an electronically muffled hole in the bulletproof glass. Her voice sounds like it is eight hundred miles away even though she is in spitting distance. She's been working for New York City for at least nineteen centuries, most definitely.

"Are you asking me a question?" I say, wishing the homeless man scratching his crotch next to the booth would stop smelling like moldy cellar onions.

The subway employee gives me eyes that say, *What do you want, B?* even though I just told her. I had heard people in New York City would be difficult. She tells me to buy my card from the machine and not from her because the city invests more in robots than in people. Then I'm supposed to take the uptown R train to the Fifth Avenue stop and ask somebody who isn't armed for directions once I get there.

I am *so* on my way. I sit down in the subway car and look at all the people who only wear really dark colors. I'm a completely captive passenger, so I read the signs above their heads. "You can have . . . beautiful, clear skin." The text appears on top of a rainbow. I wonder if I have enough money to call N-Y-C Dr. Z and have him take care of the pimple that's *still* on my chin.

Exactly twenty-two minutes later, my dreams are in front of me on the corner of Fifty-seventh Street and Fifth Avenue. Only I don't see Bloomingdale's. I'm standing in front of a different New York icon. I am at Tiffany's.

I'm seething. I feel like moshing.

I was going to go to Tiffany's *tomorrow*; Bloomingdale's *needs* to be today. I do not like when things fail to go my way. I mutter foul words.

A thirty-something woman in Italian heels overhears and says, "And you think you have problems *now*." Things are starting off disorganized.

The subway ticket woman sent me to the wrong store. And this one doesn't even sell clothes! I am lost, but I can still stand here and look mean like the other locals on Fifth Avenue. I make the *grrrr* sound in my head because I believe I will look invincible so no one will stick me up with a semiautomatic weapon.

Grrrr-ing makes me thirsty, so I head to a street vendor.

"How much is that Sprite?" I give him the doe eyes that have gotten me into and out of trouble before. I know that makes me a dough-head, but free is free, and there's a lot of dough to be saved in that.

"Two dollars." He doesn't even look at me. I mutter and mutter. "Hey, stop that," he says with a Latin accent. "I have delicate ears. Why does such pretty, petite little senorita need to say such dirty words?"

"Oops."

"Just give me one doll*air*." He does not look dirty like the hot dog man did. I hand him a bill and wink and tell him to have a nice day. Unlike most people, I mean it.

73

I decide to make the best of things. After all, it's not so bad to be standing in front of Tiffany's with black satin gloves on. It's just that I had hoped to make this a Very Big Deal. Soon, when I was no longer afraid of armed pigeons, I planned to come here to pay homage to Nina and Holly Golightly and Audrey Hepburn, *Breakfast at Tiffany's* style. I was going to wear the same little black dress I have on now, only clean, and eat a pastry while drinking coffee on the sidewalk by the Fifth Avenue window.

Landing here could be a sign. But of what? That things aren't going to go as I plan them? Or that my luck is as great as a little blue box wrapped in white ribbon?

Oh, drat. I'm overthinking.

I have to wait in line to get through the revolving entrance doors of the marble and sterling silver store.

The security guard says, "Hello, welcome to Tiffany," and I have what I need for this moment.

I realize my emotions are up and down like a yo-yo, but I don't need a mood-stabilizing prescription; I just need to sleep. Then I remember what Nina used to tell me: "Stay up now and sleep when you die."

"Where's the biggest diamond you have?" I ask a

man with a pencil-thin mustache who hocks platinum-band watches.

"Fourth floor." The guy points with an insensitive left finger and continues to polish something that already shines. But I stand there long enough to make him notice. "What?" he asks.

"Look. At me."

He puts down a cleaning cloth that is, of course, Tiffany blue, and his gaze is on me for ten whole seconds.

"Thanks." It was Nina who told me that all you have to do is make the request.

"No problem." He has spiky hair for an older man. He bites his bottom lip, and that's when I notice he's wearing a slightly pink-tinted lip gloss. He shakes his head in an ever-so-slight approving way, and I'm reminded again to make this dress in more colors. The salesguy sighs dramatically with a lisp.

And just like that, he picks up his cloth again. The moment is over, and he goes back to work while he speaks to me. "So, you're one of those, huh?"

"One of what?"

"Like you don't know. When you get to the fourth floor, walk all the way to the back and to the right.

Make sure you ask for Thomas, dear. He'll be pleased to meet you."

I follow these directions and approach a man with a shiny head and pudgy face in the back not paying attention to his diamonds. I pay attention to him, though. He is wearing a skinny beige plaid suit.

"Is that Vivienne Westwood?" I ask. "Circa nineteen seventy-nine?"

His eyebrows raise, and I just *know*. Vivienne Westwood is this really important designer who's awesome even if she is too funkified for me personally. He checks out my dress, but he doesn't show approval or dislike.

"I want to see a big diamond." I reach into my backpack and show him my sketchbook and the high-waisted deep purple fifties-but-modern dress stuffed inside that needs serious ironing. He looks, nods, and pulls out a yellow diamond pendant the size of a Splenda packet.

My eyes turn to flying saucers. His roll up toward the top of his head. Nothing impresses this guy, not even the magnificent jewelry he sells.

I put my head down closer to it. "But I want so much more than that."

"That's why we are here," he answers. Now he's pleasant-faced; I wouldn't dare call that a smile. His cheeks are rosy, and he's not wearing blush, I don't think.

I have secret ways of getting boys, even boys not interested in girls, to warm up. "May I?" I ask, pulling out a box of Cracker Jacks I got from Trucker Hat.

"Only if you give me a handful," Thomas says as I take off my black gloves and pour carefully so I don't give him the prize.

I am standing in Tiffany's in front of a yellow diamond eating my afternoon snack with a man in a vintage Vivienne Westwood suit. My mind wanders off to something about luck and being alive. *This is homage enough, Nina and Holly. But I'll give you more.* I eat the sweet popcorn first and save the salty peanuts for last.

"So, what'd you get?" Thomas asks, knowing exactly when to let me think and when to interrupt.

I am careful when I open the little red-and-blue paper packet prize that I'd been trying to keep hidden. It is just a sticker for little kids, but nirvana, sugar, and overstimulation have me thinking the prize is even more beautiful than the yellow diamond that's sparkling at me. If you look at the sticker one way, it's a picture of a wide-eyed bald guy with a trembling expression. Turn it upside down, and the sticker appears to be a bug-eyed bald guy with a gnarly mouth. I like the latter better because I'm into gnarly mouths. I place the sticker on the left side of my dress.

Thomas leans over the counter trying to read it. He squints dramatically when he mouths the words, "I'm . . . so . . . tough. . . ." He looks at me north and south and giggles.

I stick out my tongue, telling myself to keep my middle fingers calmly at my sides. I am not into being mocked. I take off my sticker and slap it down on his glass counter right next to the diamond.

"Tell me this," Thomas says, leaning his bony arms on the counter he'd just been cleaning. "Why are you here? *Really?*"

I lean way into him, and I start a standoff. Our eyes are two inches apart, and it occurs to me that we have the same shade of dirty blue.

"I . . . don't . . . know." I'm really being serious.

"Yes, you do. What do you want? Only certain types come to the fourth floor and ask for me."

We are still eye to eye. I start to back away so I can think of how best to answer his question.

"Come on, you're not the kind of girl to step off." He points to his eyes and then to my eyes. I lean back in.

"I want to get my stuff, like stuff I make, in Bloomingdale's because I promised someone I love that I would. I want to be a fashion designer, a real one, or I might as well give up and get a job at Whole Foods right now." I stop talking to think hard, and I look him in the eye without really looking at him. I'm looking into myself — and I'm seeing so much that my heart feels like holes. "Bloomingdale's has a contest, for the very best teens who sew and design. *The VERY best teens.* And I bet you know about it. I have to start over. I need to be me but with a new identity and a high school diploma. I need to find a friend, a real one. I want someone not related to me to see my work and love it. I need that. Oh, and it would be nice to lose my virginity again, but love is last on the list. Getting over Muddy is higher."

I don't tell him about the paralyzing sense of loss that weighs on my shoulders.

"Good." The yellow diamond is still gleaming, off

to his left side. He doesn't even keep watch over it while he listens and talks to me. "I'm in the graduate program at FIT. In jewelry design. Yes, of course I know about the Bloomingdale's contest. Also, a friend of mine at school teaches a great TV-show-inspired fashion class for teens that you'll love — and rumor has it that she's making everyone enter The Line. But she's picky; she only takes top talent."

"Her definition of top is my bottom." I stand up tall.

"I mean she only takes teens performing at peak." He is squinting at me.

"Think of me this way: If there were a Mount Everest in sewing, I have climbed it." I am not angry that he's questioning me; I like that I have to prove myself to a real New Yorker. Bring on the aggression.

"Can you do a corset?" He's acting bored now, totally over me.

"In one day." Okay, so maybe it takes me more like twenty-eight hours with absolutely no stopping to sleep, eat, or wee. And that doesn't include shopping for my fabric.

Now his eyes widen, and his contact pops over a little so I can see his blue eyes are really brown. *Hee, bee.* He gets himself together, acts snotty again, and adds, "Then take her class. I mean, you'll more than love it. It will change your life. And here . . ." He fiddles in his pocket for a silver — Tiffany's — business card holder. He writes e-mail addresses and phone numbers on the back. "Call this guy about your identity."

"Oh, thank God, I found some guy from Queens online. He was going to meet me and help me with a new Social Security card and a fake high school diploma and all of that. But I've been worried he was going to kidnap me. This guy won't?" I'm standing here wondering if I maybe exaggerated too much about my corset-making abilities.

He glares at me in a way that tells me he's more fabulous than I'll ever be, and I better not question his judgment.

I continue: "*Thank you.* But what about the friends and virginity, and, like, a place to stay?" I made a note to self about how I better work on *never* seeming needy, or I'll never get what I need.

"How much money do you have?" He's scanning the room now, sending me a signal that's he's bored with me. New Yorkers — hmph.

"Enough. I think."

84

"The people who come into Tiffany are of two types financially: your average tourist or rich. Which one are you?" He speaks over my head, looking at someone else. But he doesn't shake my confidence.

"I will be rich in December if my mother doesn't sue me. Right now, I'm not rich. But even when I am, I will be frugal. My absolute maximum is as much as I am allowed to withdraw from the bank, and that's five a day, but I'm trying to live on quite a bit less." I am computing it all as best I can.

"Five thousand?" He scratches his head with longish fingernails. Ouch.

"Five hundred." I'm seriously embarrassed and feeling stupid. I'm guessing that most girls who come here are truly loaded and not just spawn of drip-coffee-machine makers like me. I scratch my head with my nubby fingernail. *Red nail polish chipped? Nope. Cool.*

He laughs, but this time it's gentler, not so mocky mocky. "Relax. Ever heard of the Chelsea Hotel?"

"No."

"Sid and Nancy?"

"Is that a brand of oatmeal?"

He huffs loudly, and a Tiffany's security guard tells him to keep it down. I'm feeling so very stupid because I've obviously said something wrong, and I'm trying to be so very right. I scratch my thigh and roll my eyes and act over it. I think I'm accidentally scratching my butt.

"Don't be a cliché. Just go to the front desk, ask for Stanley Bard, and tell him Thomas sent you. Don't even think about going until you have your samples in your hands. Like skirts and arm warmers and stuff. He only rents to artists. By the way, do you make chaps?"

"Just assless pants." I'm totally not making him or anyone else assless pants *or* chaps, not in my current lifetime. But I act serious because I don't want to offend anyone else in this city at this moment.

"You're too young to traipse around Manhattan by yourself. I'd let you stay with me if I didn't live in Queens — and watch what you say about Queens — with my very jealous boyfriend. You think you're tough," he says as he scrapes the gnarly-mouth sticker off his glass counter, "but you haven't even been on the A train yet." His head is jerking around, and I can

83

tell he's ready to move on to something else — like his work or his cell phone or some other girl.

To get me out of there in a prompt and tidy manner that matches his perfectly tailored clothing and shiny head and cooler-than-thou demeanor, he opens his superskinny cell and says hello to someone named Salvatore. He turns to me. "Kid, what's your name?"

"Why would I tell you?"

"Do you want my help or not?"

"Eat mercury."

"Just make one up, Jesus Q. Christ."

I'm standing there in a rage because *no one* can know who I am, I don't care how many yellow diamond pendants and historic hotels they have access to. I'll sleep in a rat-infested Dumpster in Central Park before I'll let Hogzilla — or anyone else — find me. I start to walk off.

"Her name is Cat," he says into his phone, laughing and waving me to come back.

"How very clever of you." He's smart; I think he gets me. I stop shaking, getting control of the aggression inside that I can't explain. He hands me the business card with phone numbers, names and addresses written on the back.

"Cat *what*, dear? And this time don't give me the attitude."

"Cat Zap." This rolls out of my mouth, my homage to Betsy. "Wait, it's Zappe, with two Ps and an E."

That's when I spot three teenage girls with real New Yawk accents coming our way. They're flashing all their cards in a row, and I'm talking AmExes, Visas, *and* Mastercards. They are who he's been eyeing, so I try not to look. Acting over things has worked for me in the past.

The one with the nicest highlights picks out a necklace with a sapphire, charges it, and sighs to her drop-dead-beautiful friends. The three of them look like models who could be in commercials. But Nice Highlights is the one Thomas watches. Me, too — I have to admire her pink pencil skirt and crisp white shirt. The outfit is sixties inspired, exquisitely crisp and tailored.

"I'm bored," Nice Highlights says, rolling her eyes and turning to her friends. "Let's go to Bloomingdale's."

Thomas locks the big diamond back up dismissively and starts talking to them. "Hey, babycakes! I thought that was you. Opal, come over here and give Thomas a hug."

The two share a showy plastic embrace right in front of me, even though the security guard tells them to "pipe down."

"You're the only reason I come here," the pencil skirt girl says as they discuss jewelry design. "Check out my friends — they made their clothes, too. Do you think they can attend?"

"No way," he whispers back, and I am truly shocked that he can, in fact, keep his voice down. I eventually stop paying any attention because she looks way too young to know anything about anything. She's my age. And her friends have on woefully-made outfits with unfinished hems, off necklines and painful seams.

Thomas does not introduce us, and this is the perfect time for me to sneak out. I don't say good-bye because I hate good-byes. And, anyway, I'll be back.

"So, at Bloomingdale's," Thomas says to the girl for the whole fourth floor to hear, "you need to see Joslyn on the second floor; she'll give you the employee discount on whatever you need. Yes, even Marc by Marc." Then I hear him saying something about a place called Forty Carrots, which sells plain frozen yogurt that's not sweet. That sounds good to me, but I've got to go.

I have sewing to do, phone calls to make, and an identity to create.

I even have someone to see.

This is Chapter Nine.

I take the R train to the Prince Street station, which is supposed to be close to Greene Street where it crosses Broome. This is where a guy whose name I don't even know lives. He wrote the address down on a Post-It that's fixed to my sketch pad.

Sixty-seven Greene, I learn, is on the right-hand side of the street, and it is west of Broadway, not east, and if I go all the way to West Broadway (which is, cruelly, not the same as Broadway), I will know I've missed where I'm supposed to be. This is according to the nice man at the deli who wears a turban — there's enough fabric on his head to make a cute round skirt.

"What the heaven?" I say as I stand outside a gray door that's covered with incoherent red, pink, and black spray-painted lines of graffiti. I pull out my used iZone camera, a mini instant that takes dark-looking stamp-sized photos. I just bought the camera off a guy on Prince Street for five dollars. It came with three rolls of film, which equals thirty pictures, and I thought that would be enough to document my time in New

York. When I was a kid, I documented my fourth-grade experience with an old camera that took real film. It was mostly kids playing I'll Smack You Back. I decide to photograph interesting stuff again because even if I tell myself I'll write about it, like in a journal, I know that I won't.

iZone Photo Number One: Punked-out door before I find out what's behind it.

I want to remember the incoherent red, pink, and black graffiti forever because those lines that point in zigzagging directions with no rhythm represent my life right now, and they will represent something different and familiar to me the next time I look at them. Or at least those lines had better stand for something else, or I've just wasted my dead grandma's money on a camera that has scuffed-up Tony the Tiger stickers on it.

89

In a former life, to me, the red line equaled stop signs and people like my English teacher who told me I was too chaotic to focus on anything meaningful. It also equaled myself because I was just pretending that I didn't believe him.

In a former life, the pink equaled cheerleaders and drama students and debate team members who invited me to their parties but would've freaked if I had actually shown up during my ultra-indie/super-lonely sophomore and junior years. I take a deep long sigh that hurts somewhere down in the pit of my lungs.

In a former life, the black equaled my loved ones, one big hole because my mother likes procreating but she doesn't like kids, and if she had money she'd have shipped me off on a one-way ticket to Antarctica. She kept me around because if I was there, Nina would share her money. She kept me around because her shrink friends would have freaked if she'd actually abandoned me. She kept me around because I mostly wasn't there — Nina's Victorian dream house was just a mile away.

90

The red, pink, and black become streaks when the door blasts open, almost making me drop my camera.

I look up and the door is no longer in front of me — a young skinny guy is instead. "You will not believe what I just pulled out of my belly button!" he yells.

It's been four hours — one trip to Tiffany's, two subway rides, two Sprites, and one major freak-out when my vintage Mary Jane almost collided with a crippled pigeon — since I last talked to Trucker Hat. I am at his apartment in Soho. The name sounds like a row of front-loading Laundromat washing machines. But the neighborhood is hardly hard up. I just passed a store, something called Vivienne Tam, and mesh Buddha T-shirts were four hundred dollars a pop. My mouth waters. If people here will pay that, I can make any kind of mesh or Buddha or T-shirt they want.

I think his place is considered a loft. From what I can see from the entrance, it's sprawling, neat, and white like a GAP store, but in a gritty, artsy way. I see naked plastic baby dolls in buckets all over the place. Most of them have heads.

My heart aches. Nina would totally dig this space. She'd put our sewing room to the left where I now see a rusty metal desk. Our vintage clothes could hang in the back by the terra-cotta-tinted tile. We'd park her Vespa in the courtyard I can see through the back wall-length windows.

"What? Is my breath bad?" he asks me. We are standing within body-heat distance again. He looks down at his size twenty-two red shoes. "Oh, of course."

He is not wearing his Shins T-shirt anymore. He is dressed like Bozo the Clown in a one-piece footed outfit that's white with jumbo-sized candy-apple-red dots. He is really tall and thin, if I remember correctly, but the uniform makes him look pudgy.

I can't focus. I haven't eaten anything in hours. But that's probably not why I feel so dizzy and confined. I step out of the apartment, through the huge gray metal door with graffiti on it, to peek down the street and get some warm-thick New York City air. I see groups of Asian teens in Roberto Cavalli and pale skinny girlz and boyz in Banana. I see a cute eatery called Café Café four doors down.

The apartment is Nina.

The clown is mother-loving creepy.

I'm not scared.

I'm not terrified.

I don't love or hate clowns, actually. It's just that whenever I see one in person or on TV, I wind up having this dream where I'm vacuuming in scuffed-up Tevas while the queen of England tells dirty jokes. It's disturbing. Anyway, earlier today, he told me that since I already stole his breakfast, I might as well come down and steal his dinner, too. This option sounded good to me since I had absolutely no better options, but I hope he serves something besides clown food, and I hope he serves it in something besides a clown outfit. Visions of Cheet-o ice cream and brownie pizza do not dance merrily in my head.

He follows me out to the metal steps in front of the metal door. "Come in. I promise not to talk about my belly button."

"No, really. Your belly button is fine. Let's discuss it." I try to act normal.

Normal, like nothing strange is happening.

I have arrived in a strange city with no place to go but a strange hotel some stranger at Tiffany's recommended. I am standing in a strangely stylish neighborhood talking to a strange teenager wearing a horrifically cute red plastic nose. I picture myself thrown lifeless into the Hudson River, poodle-shaped balloons tied to my wrists and ankles.

The zit on my chin is definitely not healing tonight. Good thing I wrote down the phone number of Dr. Z.

This is the first time I question myself — or maybe it's the thousandth, I can't remember.

1. Was it really necessary to steal Muddy's money out of his glove box?

2. Did I really need to leave my mother a note saying to bite my black toenail polish because I was
leaving for good?

3. Did Nina have to leave me in this situation?
Where did she possibly have to go that was so
much more important?

I feel like stealing something, destroying something, creating something. If I do anything bad, I
wonder a) Do they get MTV2 in federal prison? b)
Why on earth did I donate my jeans, earmuffs, DVDs,
and television set to the Goodwill because I didn't
think I'd have room for them here? c) Will I wish I had
those things once I'm stuck in solitary confinement
for the rest of my natural-born life?

"You need to relax." He manages to guide me back
into the apartment, where I breathe easier than I did
outside on Greene Street. "Can I take your backpack?"
He reaches into his clown pocket and checks his cell
phone.

"Goodness no." I'm really nailing my Southern
accent now, if you ask me.

"Why? I'm not Clepto the Clown." He looks
annoyed, but not at me, at his cell, which is going off.
His ring tone is "The Oompa Loompa Song" from *Willy*

Wonka and the Chocolate Factory, which I love. He barks into the sleek device: "Yes, that's right. I will. I hate that it happened, too. Yes, I love you." He snaps it shut quite harshly. It's an innocent cell phone, geez.

"*Oompa Loompa?*" I act like I wasn't just interested in his phone call.

"Can't you see I'm a clown? I just came from a party filled with four-year-olds that I was five minutes late for. It's been a long day." He leads me back through one little room and two big ones. The huge white walls are covered with art that is made of the nude plastic babies. There is very little furniture except in the very first room by the door and the very last room, which is the terra-cotta-tiled kitchen. He jumps up a few stairs to a little room that must be his. I can hear zippers and clothes rustling. Thank heaven he is changing so I don't have to think about Tevas and vacuum cleaning. He yells down to me: "How old are you?"

"Twenty."

"You're, like, fourteen if you're lucky."

I am highly offended. Okay, maybe I don't look twenty, but I don't look like a middle-schooler, either. I mean, I have boobs. Big ones. Bs. "I'm almost out of

95

high school, and I don't see why you need to know anything other than that."

"Are you at least eighteen?"

"Are you?"

"No." I hear him stumble, like he's throwing the shoes against the walls.

I am mesmerized by the paintings in the furniture-less rooms that I just passed through. They are as big as walls, some of them, with rainbows of DNA strands. Another is Jesus's face, only deconstructed so he looks like a terrorist; others are of the babies. It's totally bright and cheerful.

"I'm nineteen," I say.

"In whose dreams?" His cell phone falls down the steps. He comes down, too, but he leaves it there, ringing.

"I'm seventeen, and that's no lie." I pick up his cell when it finally goes silent. He doesn't seem to mind when I use it to leave a message for someone named Sal. "Do you clown a lot?"

"All the time. I'm seventeen, too, by the way, thanks for asking."

"Did you paint all this art?" I am standing back in

the room with just white and paintings and a concrete floor and a weird angular wooden chair.

"No, my dad did. He'll be back tonight, or next month, or never hopefully. I don't know. He's still at our house in the Adirondacks." He is standing with me, looking at the paintings as if he's never seen them before. Which is a little weird, since he lives here.

"With your mom?" I don't know why I'm being nosy — I don't care so much about family situations.

"Only if she's unlucky. He's a typical artist — a genius megalomaniac alcoholic. I get my sense of humor from him. What's with all the questions?" Now he's walking toward the kitchen. Yum. "My mom is in the Hamptons most of the time. We live here and there, but I stay here more than I go there. I go to school and work and stuff in Manhattan. I wanted to stay here this summer to clown around."

"What's for dinner?" I ask. I don't follow him; I stay firmly planted where I am.

"Sushi. I dig your accent, where are you from really?" He's popping open a can of something, soda or maybe more cheap Pabst Blue Ribbon beer. Clearly he can afford expensive drinks, but maybe he's slumming for street cred. A lot of people do that, like poor people who wear gold teeth and rich people who shop at dollar stores.

"Savannah, Georgia."

"Hmmm." He's thinking about believing me. I see he's drinking a Sprite. I walk into the kitchen, open the fridge and grab one of my own. "Why did you come here?"

"To eat your sushi and leave."

He's standing so close. So very close. I'm trembling. He's super cute when he's cleaned up and de-clowned. Now he's unlike Muddy except for his deep brown eyes. He's stylish and chic but slumming, prissy-boy style, and talking like he's big-city smart. He's clean, yep. No face paint, no ear wax, no odd breath. He smells like cucumbers and spice.

I tell him I'm staying at the Chelsea Hotel, and he says his dad has a friend who lives there. Clearly, he approves. Our dinner arrives from a small man on a bike with a metal basket in the front. My new New York City unfriend unpacks the fresh fish and tells me his name: "Adrian Ashbaugh. What's yours?"

"Cat. What's your clown name?"

"Mr. Giggles." He's a less-geeky Luke Skywalker.

Trucker Hat is alterna-hot, and not in that suicidal, self-hating, lurpy emo way. He's earnest but not syrupy. He's cynical but not dark.

"Adrian . . . Ashbaugh . . . Giggles . . . Big A . . . Skinny G . . . G Dog. I don't like those. You had that hat on the bus today. Can I just call you Trucker?" I love names that aren't really names because then you can tell a lot more about a person. We inch farther back into the apartment, into the terra-cotta kitchen with big windows.

"Call me whatever you want. Then both of our names will be made up. I bet you're an Elizabeth or maybe a Jessica. Laura?"

"It's Cat Zappe. Believe whatever. So, tell me, what is in your belly button?" I'm still kind of nervous, and that irritates me because I'm not nervous often.

"A key." He turns around and pretends he's pulling something out of his stomach. It's totally goobery but funny. He reaches it my way, but he doesn't let go of it that easily.

"To what?"

"This apartment. Only for emergencies."

"You're trusting," I say as the key falls on the floor. He picks it up and, strangely, doesn't hand it to me.

"Not really. I just don't want to see some seventeen-year-old Southern girl out on the mean streets even though she's crazy and probably deserves to be." I can't tell if he's being serious or making fun of me. Or if this is really all about something else he's not mentioning. He has this way of giving a smirky expression that doesn't mean anything. But his hair flops over to the side softly, and I will believe anything he says for now.

"Or maybe you want me to trash your dad's place." I certainly know all about wanting revenge on a parent. He doesn't seem too keen on his, either. "Do you two not get along?"

"I don't particularly care for raging megalomaniac alcoholics who stuff my car keys in our toilet. Didn't I already tell you that? Don't get me wrong — I don't care. I'm over it. My mom is pretty cool, at least." He's not looking my way; he's not giving me any expression to analyze. His tush is tight, though.

"I know all about being over it. I am planning to go to the Chelsea, but I will take your key. I suspect, however, there's something else you want from me."

"You're right." Now he is looking at me — like seriously.

"Crap." I don't want to dance topless or do anything that involves flesh. But I don't let him see me flinch. "Whatever it is, my underwear stays *on*."

"Shame on you. What kind of guy do you think I am? Look, my girlfriend usually does this job, but she's too bipolar lately. My good friend Bailey helped me today, but his beard and fat really scared the kids. How about you come to Soho House and help me with a one-year-old's birthday party next weekend? What else do you have to do?" He's playing with the soft drink can, sitting down at the stainless steel kitchen table.

I plop my weary bum onto the cold concrete floor in the other room, the white one, underneath terrorist Jesus. I am so tired, way too tired to think. He has a girlfriend? Being a clown in exchange for a key and a maybe-friend? "Sure." Then I realize why he was nice to me in the Port Authority. He saw the clown in me from the beginning.

Nothing is ever free, Nina always reminded me.

"You can say hi to the kids and help me tie balloons." He is sitting down next to me now, and he looks less like Muddy all the time. Muddy is a guy's guy. He likes to build things and not shave and watch

Cops. Trucker likes to shop — his jeans are Sevens — and I bet he watches shows on Bravo. "I need a girl there so I don't seem like a perv, which I'm not. Anyway, it's not really from my belly button, but here." He stands up to reach in his pocket for the key, and he gives me his cell phone number. I remind myself to get a new cell of my own with a New York number that no one knows. I wonder if Muddy has texted my dead phone. I've wanted to text him a thousand good and evil thoughts. For now, I will wait and rely on pay phones, which are surprisingly difficult to find.

I hear "The Oompa Loompa Song" on his cell again.

Oompa loompa doompadee do
I've got a perfect puzzle for you.

"You're doing what? They're not midgets, they are little people," Trucker is yelling into the mouthpiece. "You need help, Marni. This is why we talked about time apart the other day. I cannot help you anymore." I sneak out with my backpack and a Sprite. There is pain in his voice, and the words *spin, spin, buzz, buzz* come to mind. I have been ignoring the way my heart aches and the person I miss. If I don't get to my hotel and tend to it now, things are going to get dark and stormy.

"Where are you going?" he says to me, holding his hand over the mouthpiece. I can hear a girl's voice screaming through the phone. Then he screams back: "No, I am not!"

He's involved in a relationship crisis, and I can't even get in the words, *see ya soon*. So I think them instead, and I slip out the pink, red, and black graffiti door. On my way to the Chelsea Hotel, I make myself not think about anything but this.

What exactly does a female clown assistant wear?

This is Chapter Ten.

Summer Live Fashion Design Course for Exceptional High School Students at the Fashion Institute of Technology in the Heart of Manhattan's Artistic Community of Chelsea and Just South of the World-Renowned New York City Garment District.

This is the class Thomas's friend teaches, and it is where I belong. It starts tomorrow, Monday. That's way too soon but I'm pretty lucky it didn't start *last* Monday when I was still mapping out my entire future. I *have* to get in that class even though the online description says it's full. I have her number. I just need to call but my cell is somewhere in the middle of Interstate 87.

A class will give me structure. I love structure. Nina and I were both happiest when we had purpose. For example, partying recklessly was forbidden — her parties were for charity or networking or saying thank you. When I partied hardest during eighth grade and freshman year, it was for improving my DJ skills and my tolerance for beverages, neither of which ever became any better.

So first thing tomorrow, I will head to FIT at Twenty-seventh Street and Seventh Avenue. Is that north of here? South? Wait, where am I again? I'm already in Chelsea since this place is called the Chelsea Hotel. I'm on Twenty-third Street, so it can't be more than ten blocks away. Maybe twenty.

I don't think I belong where I am. This is a fleabag hotel — seriously flea-y. There is no mini-bar, no bellhop, no electronic key. Not that I need any of that stuff — I just thought some things were standard in places that charged by the night. But this isn't even really a hotel because I heard in the elevator that there are actual residents here` among the guests like me. Even the walls are battered — plaster is cracked, wallpaper is torn. I hear this place is famous, but what for? Fleas and funny-looking people? And what did Sid do to Nancy? I dare not ask. This hotel dude named Stanley already emphasized that I was an insurance risk, and that he shouldn't rent to seventeen-year-olds, and that Thomas had better stop sending him homeless girls with credit cards.

I need my Nina.

Instead of sitting here trying not to cry, I concentrate on what I have accomplished so far. I *am* in New

York City, and that makes my insides flicker. And I did it almost by myself with a special thanks to Thomas from Tiffany's and to Trucker from Soho, both of whom give great subway directions.

It is Sunday night, and I plan to sit in this peculiar lobby in New York City until someone throws me out. I like the paintings that reach out for me from every direction. There's a twice-as-large-as-life horse perched above my head. I like the sound of the street through the glass front doors. I even like the greenish-gold velour seat my butt is in. I pretend it doesn't smell funny, because it's comfy.

I like the people walking around — ancient and creative and corpselike with paint splattered on their overalls. The guy to my right has a feather coming out of the exact middle of his head. The woman to my left has seriously brassy hair and surgically enhanced lips. The youngest occupants are like twenty, and they're wearing full black leather even though this is Sunday, July 14. The smell of warm herbs rains down on us from the second floor. I know that scent from Nina's wilder parties, though I was never into smoking.

I want to yell out: *Yes, you are cooler than I will ever be.* I want to yell this to everyone in earshot, including all of New York City. Instead, I just sneeze, way too loudly, and I think I got some on the feather-headed dude.

A guy who introduced himself as Robert says, "Bless you."

When they look my way, what do they think? Maybe I just look like I need to buy some clothes. I wasn't trying to be weird by wearing pink chicken pajama pants and an old *CosmoGIRL!* T-shirt, gift with subscription. I was simply too tired to get dressed, and I was in a hurry to find out about FIT on this lobby Internet connection. I, um, have an ultraportable laptop that, um, belongs to Muddy. It was stuffed into my backpack, wrapped inside my purple dress. I didn't technically steal it since he was supposed to be here with me.

"Where did you get those pants?" Robert asks, and I think he's way too elderly at age thirty to be hitting on me.

"Look at that! They magically appeared on my legs today." I stare at the computer screen, and he gets my message and leaves.

It suddenly occurs to me that no matter how worn out she might be, Madeleine wouldn't wear chicken pajamas in public. Neither would Muddy or Hogzilla or Holly Golightly — or even Nina. Maybe I am different, maybe I always was different, maybe I will be different in the future despite all attempts to the contrary. The thing is — why? I don't mean to be.

So now I see why Thomas from Tiffany's sent me here. It's like he knew I had chicken pajamas in my backpack.

But in the peculiarity of this particular place, there's, like, this death vibe all around me. I don't know if it's the cast-iron spiderlike filigree designs on the spiraling infinite stairwell, or if I'm still feeling my own eulogy-related sadness. But the Chelsea Hotel feels like it could go one of two ways: ecstatic or sinister. It makes me want to mope around a goth club in white pancake makeup and vampire eyeteeth. But that's so not me. I want to be happy.

So I think I will have to get out of here. Nina's in the paintings, in the skin color of the people next to me, in the blackness of the iron that goes up a supposedly famous gothic staircase. It's like I feel her behind me in the lobby, in the tiny room Thomas called ahead and set up for me, in the bathroom

I share with two other residents for one hundred and twenty-five dollars per night. I see her gleaming in the dull marble floors. My veins are so heavy, and the reminders of her make them heavier. I thought it wouldn't hurt as bad once I arrived in the city, and at Tiffany's it let up. Here, I feel pain. Every hair follicle on my head opens wide to let the tingles in, like hair dye mixed with too much developer.

So I ask myself a question I often ask myself: *WWHD?* What would Holly do?

The answer is right there on my computer screen:

Summer Live Fashion Design Course for Exceptional High School Students at the Fashion Institute of Technology in the Heart of Manhattan's Artistic Community of Chelsea and Just South of the World-Renowned New York City Garment District.

I will be there tomorrow morning, first thing. I borrow Robert's cell phone and leave a message for the instructor. I'll just go whether she e-mails me back or not. My fingers, toes, and threads are crossed.

Tomorrow, I must do the following:

1. Get properly enrolled in the class, some way, somehow.

2. Go to Bloomingdale's after school to sign up for the contest (fudging the high school diploma requirement just a little).

3. Find a sewing machine I can use that won't break Nina's bank.

4. Make myself a decent skirt because I can't wear chicken pajamas and a little black dress every day. *I wonder where I can find decent bias tape for a cute trim?*

5. Call identity guy.

6. Find someone to help me get my boxes as soon and as cheaply as possible.

7. Try to figure out a way to stop this spinning. *Save money. Save money. You never know when you'll run out.*

I want to wear my superwrinkled purple dress to class tomorrow to make the perfect look-at-me-I'm-a-designer impression. But I don't have an iron.

I turn to Robert and sigh before smiling sweetly and saying, "Hey, I need to borrow something."

This is Chapter Eleven.

I am happy as I walk into FIT at Twenty-seventh Street and Seventh Avenue. The names and numbers of streets are pretty confusing. Some go east, others go south. I find my way surprisingly well with my foldout map despite my gruesome sense of direction.

And there it is. The Marvin Feldman Center at FIT is in front of me, just through those doors. I am here! It is real. This is the Fashion Institute of Technology, a place where fashion history is made. Just when I think things can't possibly go better, I see something that I can hardly believe. Some things, many things, are too good to be true, like this sign taped onto the glass entryway. It's printed on bright pink paper with underground zinelike script.

ENTER THE FINISHED LINE!!!

Want to be the next Heatherette or Proenza Schouler? If you're entering a NYC-area college in the fall, and you have a passion for fashion, this competition is for you. *CosmoGIRL!* and Bloomingdale's offer the winner:

*$5,000 toward your college education

*$5,000 toward your clothing line

*A fashion internship at *CosmoGIRL!* fall semester and a design internship at Bloomingdale's for spring semester.

*One of your winning pieces will be sold at Bloomingdale's this fall under *your* label!

Either alone or in teams of two, submit your collection, three ready-to-wear pieces by Wednesday, July 24, to the *CosmoGIRL!* coordinator in the registrar's office. (email <u>info@finishedline.org</u>). Winners will be announced at an evening fashion show at Bloomingdale's, Lexington Ave., Wednesday, July 24. To be eligible, you *must* be a high school graduate, enrolling in college either fall or winter semesters. Judges will be *CosmoGIRL!*'s editor-in-chief, Bloomingdale's head designer, and the assistant chair of fashion design with the Fashion Institute of Technology.

I rip down the sign and fold it up as small as it will go, tucking it into my bra next to Nina's handwritten good-bye note with its detailed, numbered instructions for living the rest of my life. My boobs are getting itchy with all the paper, but I'm doing anything and everything I can for good luck. I walk into the hall and tear off another sign, but that's probably not good karma, so I try to put it back.

As I'd hoped, when I walk into the classroom, I see stylish teenagers. It doesn't have to be *my* style; I just admire style. Some are architect types in tight black clothes with thick plastic glasses. An Eastern European is ghetto fabulous, complete with nine-inch airbrushed nails and gold grills, a few Asian girls in Anna Sui and Miu Miu gather around her. I love the gay guy who wears a bandanna and a skirt — he's into purple and red and orange. A brown-skinned girl talks to him in her Lily Pulitzer palm tree pants. There are also a few Chanel-wannabe queens. A vampire empress sits in the corner rocking out to silence. I am enlightened by everyone — the punks, goths, mods, gays, super-straights, preps, freaks. No one is updated sixties-chic-Holly-on-punk like me — big huge sigh of immense relief for individuality. I sit in the desk behind a girl dressed all eighties rock 'n' roll in the corner with multicolored hair.

The only thing that worries me is the teacher,

Kera Sahn. She dresses hippie with jingle-jangle anklets (does she really need seven?) and too-long hair and skirt. I had hoped for the gay fashion designer type, the guy too good to breathe unfiltered air. Dressing like you're into acid is *so* twentieth century. It's not really the hippie-loving aura around her that bugs me. I think it's the fact that her dress hem isn't finished and her T-shirt collar isn't straight. She obviously made her clothes, and they obviously are not well made.

I worry more. The teacher goes on to say that the goal of the class is to pair with a partner and draw a collection on storyboards. She tells us to work on our color stories. This does not please me. The class is two weeks long. These exercises only take a few hours.

I want to *make* stuff like Nina and I used to do. And, most important, I want to do it on my own — in honor of her. I have to get back to my sewing; I haven't done it for four whole days. Fixing an unraveled hem on my black Holly dress on the Greyhound doesn't count. Making clothes makes me feel closer and warmer and more alive and less alone. It's like an addiction for me, *and* it's good for my health. The addictions I've had in the past — Muddy, online auctions for vintage patterns, picking fights with my feral mother — not so much.

"Can't I just produce my own clothes?" I ask, raising my hand in a hurry afterward because I am trying to be polite. "By myself?" This group thing is going to bite big time, and I don't care if I say so. I get stuck with a Type A or a Type Z, which never quite goes with my Type In-Between.

"Some of you might want to *pair up* and do that," she says, jingle-jangling around the room. Her look at me is at least softening. "Get your drawings approved by me first. We'll either show collections on board or maybe even make them if your skills are up to snuff. You want to sew, go ahead. This is your class, your money, and I'm pro-choice." She taps her pencil on things a lot, too much. She adds quietly as if she's talking to invisible ghosts, "I need to gauge the ability level of the class before making any decisions."

I didn't pay because I, um, didn't register, but I'll bring that up privately after class when I beg to get in.

The lecture on fashion as the need for tribal belonging is obvious. I would be sketching my collection — *Breakfast at Tiffany's* gone Hollywood riot grrrl, tailored but funky — but I've forgotten to bring my supplies. I kick myself for being disorganized. My to-do list is in my sketchbook, which is next to my bed on a chair because it's not like the hotel believes in providing nightstands. Or air-conditioning. Seriously. The jingle-jangle teacher starts discussing textile technology, which is really great, but I know about cotton blends (polyester plus cotton is best thread, duh!). Superwide yawn.

The teacher sees me and says, "Theory without Practice is sterile, and Practice without Theory is futile," probably directed at me. But my head is so heavy, it goes down toward the desk with the initials A.S.S. scratched into it. My eyes close, and the wonky half-awake sequence begins:

Nina has brought over Hogzilla's old wading pool. The color is a faded peach that suggests it was once the shade of a watermelon sunset. I remember liking the starfish that smiled and the whales that winked. I don't, however, like the water. My mother fills the pool with our brown and moldy backyard hose, and I don't want to touch anything that pours out of its nozzle. I don't want to suffer death by cooties.

"Get your skinny butt in there," my mother says

after I wrinkle my nose, squint my eyes, and stick my tongue out. "Your little friend doesn't mind, so why do you think you're better than him?" My little friend and next-door neighbor Toby also sticks earthworms up his nose and likes to play Pass the Dog Poo.

"Cuties," I say, my four-year-old words and meanings often gummed up.

Nina takes my hand and stands by the edge of the pool. Even though she is wearing a pair of linen shorts she's just finished hemming, she sticks her toes in, makes a *hrrr* sound with her lips, then plops down next to Toby, who splashes her right in her aviator-inspired sunglasses. She still has hold of my hand, even though my feet are firmly planted in the grass. She gives me a little tug, and I put one leg, then the other, over the cracking sides of the old plastic pool and sit down in her lap.

"Stupid girl," my mother says, her round wire-rimmed glasses sliding down her nose.

"Precious girl," Nina whispers so only Toby and I can hear. "I will help you show her who you are one day."

Then I think about how all this mess progressed. . . . My mother never wanted kids. She wanted to be a psychiatrist instead, the kind of shrink who gets a medical degree and can prescribe seriously controlled substances. But she got pregnant with me at twenty-three, like that's my fault, and she felt she had to give up plans to go to medical school. She forgot her dream of having M.D. initials officially and forever following her name. She got a job instead. By the time I was born, she already had her master's degrees in psychology and social work, so she became a therapist who, like all other therapists, thinks she's gotten herself together.

My mother is a shrink and will be until she dies. Her work is messed up, and she works around the clock. Hand her a room full of wackos and she comes alive. I'm not wacko — or maybe not wacko enough — so she never came alive around me. She always acts like I'm really boring. Clothing is "a totally artificial expression of the human spirit" and "fashion designers are promoting all that is evil and commercial in this world." Whatever. She's the one who needs Prozac and an eyebrow wax.

Hogzilla wins awards for her service with the seriously mental ill in upstate New York. With the mentals, she's helpful, kind, generous, giving, and understanding. With me, my hair is too long, so I cut it, and she tells me it's too short. I clean the kitchen but she'll say the Pine-Sol makes her sick even though that's what she bought for me to use. She tells me I'm getting pudgy. I work out, and then she hands me studies published in *JAMA* about the dangers of body dysmorphic disorder. When I was still in middle school, I'd try to hug her, but she'd always stop me and make me wash my hands first. I haven't tried to touch her again, and the only time she hugged me since was at Nina's funeral, and I pushed her away.

I'm not a shrink, I'm a fashion designer. I don't always understand terms like *manic, borderline,* or *addict.* But I do know absolutely for sure that she's clinically mean and crazy. To justify being mean and crazy, she's out to save the public world without worrying about her private one.

Nina said I look just like her, and she looks just like Nina. Hard to believe I could be more mature than they were sometimes. Nina with her parties; Hogzilla with her men; me with my curfews for both of them. My dad says so, too. His name is Greg, and he calls me twice a year — on Christmas and on my birthday, which are just a few weeks apart. He calls my mother Paula Bunyan because she wields her smiles and her axes often. He married her for, like, five minutes when she was pregnant. But he's a smart man, an economics professor, and he knew that his intense lust for her would only lead to lifelong misery. He left her in the middle of the night after a huge fight about whether to purchase Ragu or Prego. I guess they had a lot of fights. I was way too little to remember them together, but I know she loved him best. He lives in Pittsburgh with his nice wife and their three kids. The last time I visited, two years ago, I vowed not to go back. For all of their dysfunction, they are more functional than the family I've grown up with. I always had the option to live in Pittsburgh, but I didn't want to leave Nina alone with her daughter. I love Nina dearly even while she's dead.

It was safer at her place, which was one mile from my mother's. My mom often rents the basement to her favorite wackos who have supposedly completed their recovery. Various phobics, with names like Smokey and Zip, live down there. Not even her three husbands could compete with her OCD on psychology. When bachelor number four moved in two years ago — that's when I knew I'd run away for real. Russ.

Yuck. He says my mom is hotter than Natalie Wood and Natalie Portman put together, and that's what he likes best about her, so they have the healthiest unhealthy relationship I've seen yet. It's physical and nothing more, but that's exactly as much as either one of them can handle.

Nina and I could handle anything — we'd just sew or, if we were tired, we'd just watch *Breakfast at Tiffany's* or sometimes *Buffy the Vampire Slayer* — together.

This disorganized, messy, and all-true dream sequence jumps around, too, as I begin to dream within the dream that Nina and I are standing in front of Tiffany's. I'm holding the coffee with cream and sugar. She's holding the pastry that we are about to share. We're both wearing large dark sunglasses and sherbet tracksuits. We are walking into Tiffany's together. . . .

CLUNK. *Clunk. Clunk. Clunk.* My desk is vibrating.

I've built a drool pool on my desk. My brow bone is comfortable against the old-school wood desktop. I hear the cigarette-singed voice of my teacher waning prophetically about the joys and frustrations of working with one-hundred-percent cotton. God, I learned that in first grade when I tried to make a jumper out of knit instead of woven, and I don't know how I'll ever stay awake for two weeks. I just want to make my clothes and win a contest and be a famous fashion designer. I just hoped this class would give me the structure I need to reach my goals. Thomas had said it would.

CLUNK. Clunk. Clunk. Clunk. Clunk.

"*What?*" I turn around and say too loudly to the girl with red, purple, and pink streaks in her hair.

"Wake up, dude." She's wearing a pink Izod with a frog-green mini mini with lace-up boots. Her glasses are thick black plastic. Her hair is supercolorful but probably blond underneath the dye. After she finishes twirling pink bubble gum around her finger, she asks: "Did you hear that?!" Her butt comes up off the seat; she is all worked up.

"Huh, what?" I have definitely messed up my shiny Tutti Fruiti lip gloss, my hair, and my purple dress. I didn't mean to sleep that hard. I wish I hadn't — the things I dream are exactly the things I'm trying so hard to escape. Doesn't matter if I ditch my cell phone, or even my whole life. The pain remains. "Does anyone have a Tylenol?"

I hear some rooting around, and then black fishnet-covered fingers hand me two tablets I promptly dry-gulp as this person behind me keeps talking. And talking.

"Everyone in the class wants to do an actual collection, not just boards. People in this section can *sew*! I'm so excited! Kera Sahn says —" This color-haired girl is trying to whisper but she's being loud. She's buzzing along with the others in the classroom. The young designer voices echo from the concrete-block walls of this room.

The girl continues: "Kera Sahn says her best friend Thomas at Tiffany's helped her recruit an amazing class this year, like he said he would. Do you know him? He totally got me my discount at Intermix." I can smell her gum even though she chews politely.

123

"Thomas, Tiffany's, Intermix, yeah." I could tell Thomas was an enigma. Nina had lots of friends like that. I turn around, mesmerized not by my chirpy classmate but by the girl behind me to the left, the one I cannot believe I am just now noticing. I see the blue sapphire hanging from her neck first. It's the blue of a berry, the size and shape of an African violet flower.

The Girl with Nice Highlights.

Her eyes meet mine. I do not see a pleasant expression. I would even say she's scowling, but I am paranoid. She is surrounded by two Chanel-chic-wannabes. I bet they all go to private schools that cost as much as several new Volvos.

To her left, there's a skinny black dude in tight plaid pants who seriously needs to eat food. He's going on about the quality of Japanese denim, but no one is paying attention. He has wild eyes, like a superfurry feral kitten. He is suddenly quiet, is in his own world, bobbing his head to whatever song he has lodged in it.

Aren't there, like, thirty-five million people in this city? How can this be?

It's like she's reading my mind. Her name, of course, is Opal, and Opal is aggressive. She walks up to my desk and says, "Thomas says *you* are the one to watch out for. Hmph." And just like that, she walks off.

My striped-hair classmate says to me: "Who's that? What happened? Why so uptight?"

"Watch this." I get up and walk two desks over to Opal's, prying through the two Channel-chic-wannabes. *No one, and I do mean no one, hmphs and walks away from me.*

"Hello, Opal. My name is Cat." I have a very serious

expression that I got from studying the reporters on CNN.

"I know." Opal's big fat fake smile is stereotypical fashion designer-y. "Whatever."

"Whatever me again and you'll wear that sapphire in your eye. Got it? Now go back to Wal-Mart." I turn on point and walk off.

"Meow, meow." The skinny gay guy is clapping, his head following us back and forth.

I whisper to him that this isn't the U.S. Open; it's fashion class.

He is so loud when he laughs. Fat ha-ha-has come from his bones. The Chanel-wannabes stay put in the corner, whispering and looking my way. I'm not scared at all. Not one bit.

"Cat, huh?" Striped-hair neighbor has a cheery voice that has a shiny happy way of diffusing any intensity in the air. "I'm Cynthia. Want a sip of my organic sugar-free vanilla soy chai tea?"

"You look like Betsey Johnson," I say. Betsey is an important designer who started in the sixties after winning a contest by *Mademoiselle.* (!!!) She hung out with Andy Warhol and does youthquake, rock-'n'-roll, supergirlie, supercute dresses and outfits to this

125

day. Betsey freaking rules, and not just because she does a cartwheel at the end of all of her shows.

"Oh. My. God. I *worship* Betsey Johnson." Cynthia's so earnest about this, I think *she's* going to do gymnastics. She has finished her tea and gotten out her antibacterial wipes. I'm pretty sure she's seen *Annie Hall* a whole lot of times because she's so New York neurotypical. Much of her hair is crimped, and some is pulled into ponytails on the top. She's trying too hard to be cool, but who isn't? And while she'd be a total freak in Queensbury, the best thing ever is that her style choices are fine with New York City.

New York City actually cares but couldn't actually care less.

I'm trying to think while Cynthia tries to cram in as many words as possible in three seconds. "Who's your hero? Wait." There's a long pause where she twirls more bubble gum. "You have this total Audrey Hepburn look. Are you going Golightly?"

"Me? Nooooo. You think?"

"You're transparent."

I've never lived in a place — or even spent any time in a place — where I am simple. Not simple stupid, but simple as in understood. Here, I look around, and even if some of these designers are evil couture witches, they sew and design. They get it.

"Why are you pinching yourself?" Cynthia is writing down something in her sketchbook while she talks to me.

"I just want to make sure I'm not dreaming." I make a mental note to not sleep in this class anymore. I make a mental note to look studious and act alert from now on no matter how late. I stay up. I make another mental note to feed Opal to the yaks — or at least churn out better work than hers.

"Are you listening?" Cynthia asks me. "I am not putting you down for your Audrey Hepburn phase. All new designers go through it."

Wait a minute. I totally frown. I'm hissing, actually.

"Not to say you're new." She waves both of her hands, palms facing me. The skinny black dude leans toward us to listen. I can't tell if he's into me or listening in and reporting to Opal. "But maybe, well, maybe you're new to New York. There's something new about you. Anyway, I mean it as a compliment. I haven't seen Holly Golightly done so freshly. I haven't seen such a sensitive and different expression of her like I see in your purple dress. Did you make that? You had to. Like, I haven't even seen it at Bendel's, you know, and definitely not at Intermix. What I'm trying to say, and I'm not sure if it's coming out right, is this: I'm totally digging your outfit. The little black flames up the sides of that floufy fifties dress? Utter genius." My new friend (?) is easily excitable. Surprisingly, I don't feel angry anymore.

If she likes this purple dress, I've made it in four different dark colors that are in my boxes at the post office along with everything that really matters. And I can't wait to show her the funeral Holly dress in muted mod colors when I get around to making them. It's totally geeky of me, but I really have the urge to show Cynthia the vintage fabrics, yards of funky bias tape, classy piping, and the collection of clothes and patterns I have.

"So here's my idea," she adds. She has a really bouncy head, which makes it impossible not to stare at her massive amount of hair. "I want to work with you. Do you want to pair up?"

This is Chapter Twelve.

I'm on number two of my list after not properly enrolling in my class because Kera Sahn rushed out, and I couldn't pry myself from Cynthia quickly enough.She's more intense than an industrial serger. So the day is still productive, and once I get to Bloomingdale's, it can only get better.

This time I take the E train uptown to Fifty-third Street, where I switch to the uptown 6. I get off in one stop at Fifty-ninth. I am dumped out underground right next to what must be a super-secret Bloomingdale's entrance.This tiny hidden passageway into the second-most-visited site in Manhattan (thank you, guidebook) is just steps off the subway. This is an odd transition for me, a dark dingy opening into the place of my dreams.

The glass doors that say WELCOME TO BLOOMINGDALE'S are to my right. From this angle, it could be any department store at any mall anywhere. I peek past a security guard in a polyester-blend navy suit, and I see white flooring and racks. I also see a little café called Forty

Carrots. Hmmm. I do not go in. This isn't good enough.

Spin. Spin. Buzz. Buzz.

This is a great and bittersweet moment. The last time I was here I was with Nina. We came down for Fashion Week right after we'd completed a book called *Couture Sewing Techniques.* She was mastering fancy necklines and beading. She had just finished a wedding dress for her friend's daughter in Albany. It was cream with a hint of peach — we dyed the silk shantung ourselves. The dress was perfectly tailored, strapless, with only hints of beads we put on the skirt. It had a tiny train, even though we thought it looked better without it . . . but Bridezillas want what they want. I made the tiny pouf of a crinoline slip to give the skirt that princess look. Nina was teaching me everything, and I was seriously improving. She was so patient, considering the amount of time I spent chasing boys with Madeleine back then. But I still had plenty of time because life doesn't really start getting busy until you're thirteen. Anyway, we went to Bloomingdale's because we were sick of upstate bridal salons, their corsets and structure and whiteness. We just wanted to check out trendy, beautiful ready-to-wear. I definitely wanted to poach ideas from the second floor (yay!).

Back then, I lived for Juicy Couture, and we went home and made pink terry-cloth sweatsuits that matched. When I was little, I always called it Bloomie's. Nina really hated that.

"You can't nickname something so important, darling," she always said. "It diminishes its meaning." Here are some reasons why Bloomingdale's was so important to us:

1. Her old friend Baby Jane Holzer, a model, was discovered there. She was an heiress like Nina, but way more into pop culture and the Manhattan scene. Nina was, by that time, in love with my grandfather (who I never met). All the partying she did in the city definitely cost her her marriage — and probably her daughter. Anyway, Jane — who was just Jane and not Baby Jane yet — met Andy Warhol outside of Bloomingdale's, and then she became his first superstar. She was in some weird movie called *Soap Opera*. She got her start and got a big name and went on to produce

movies in Los Angeles. (She sent orchids for Nina's funeral, and I do think I saw her there.) *This is where luck happens.*

2. Jill Stuart walked into Bloomingdale's when she was fifteen years old and she showed them her line of accessories. They bought it on the spot. A few years later, in 1993, she started her own clothing label that is vintage and girlie and flirty. They gave her a chance. *This is where talent is appreciated.*

3. The A&E Channel did a *Biography* on Bloomingdale's. Other stores come and go. This is iconic. *This is where a supercool, beautiful Holly would stop first.*

132   These thoughts are all Nina's, and she ingrained them in me — just like she did with perfect seams, French hems, and other fussy finishes.

I take out a piece of cinnamon Orbit gum. Then another. The spiciness keeps me together. This was supposed to be a trip of New York City inspiration and celebration, yet it's so full of what-could've-beens that I am flipping out.

This is life. This hurts.

I go outside the store to the main entrance on

Lexington Avenue and Fifty-ninth Street. The art deco letters are in the same font as the numbers on Nina's house.

And this is where something goes wrong — me. I shake all over, but I do not cry. I fall in a heap on the sidewalk just as I'm about to go up the entrance steps, but I still do not cry. I see people flying all around me — they're getting blurry — and that's when I'm about to cry. That cannot happen, and I start to quake through my veins, through my muscles, through my skin, and even through my hair. I cannot breathe. I am blessed with the short haze of a blacked-out sleep.

As I wake a few seconds later, my body has calmed itself down. An investment banker in a black pin-striped suit and greenish button-down shirt is lightly smacking my cheeks. He looks up into the crowd that hovers around, and he says, "Someone call nine-one-one."

"Oh, stop with all of that." I sit up and thank him and assure everyone that I'm totally fine. And I am . . . for now. "It's been a long day," I say. "I'm stressed; this is not an atypical response." I stand to show everyone that I'm not a medical emergency. My legs are mush, and I want to go home, to Nina's. But that home doesn't exist. I'm going to have to make the best of it here. I *want* to make the best of it here. But where do I go?

I hear a twelve-year-old girl with a Paul Frank purse yell out, "You can *totally die* from passing out."

"The only thing that will kill me is that monkey bag you're carrying," I reply. I love Paul Frank, but that bright yellow thing just doesn't work. Still, I should've thought that instead of saying it. At least everyone promptly leaves; no one wants to stick around a meanie.

"Freak," the twelve-year-old's mother says as they scamper into the store.

The man in the black pin-striped suit — definitely Boss — stays. He asks, "With a bite like that, maybe I should call animal control." He helps me root around in my backpack to find something. I hand him the Tiffany's business card as he flicks open his cell phone.

The banker turns to me. "Your huffy friend Thomas will be right up."

This is Chapter Fourteen.[*]

So here's what happened last night. Thomas's advice was: "Babycakes, just focus. Go back to what you know."

I murmured a vulgarity along with the word no. We sat on a cosmetic-counter-sized rock in Central Park as the sun went down, only a few blocks west from my most recent scene of total embarrassment. (I bet Jill Stuart didn't pass out in front of Bloomingdale's.) We had a view of dancing roller skaters — they were blasting pop music as they glided by, fully expressing themselves. I was grateful just to sit and watch and feel the breeze and breathe easily. I snapped a little photograph with the iZone and threw it in my backpack, undeveloped.

Thomas hmphed and sighed, such a drama king. "I meant just focus on creating. On learning design. As if there's anything else."

"Fashion is crazy," I added to our comforting non-conversation. I loved the way the old roller skater

[*] Nina's superstitious nature wouldn't approve of including a chapter with the number that precedes fourteen.

with the Mohawk could twirl through the air in a three-turn edge despite his heavy shoes.

"Pure madness." There was a long pause before Thomas added, "Will you hem my pants?" Thomas had just secured a vintage Christian Dior suit, and the pants were so long that his spectator shoes didn't show at all.

"Sure," I said. I went straight to Chelsea Sewing Center, located right across the street from my haunting hotel. I bought a new Singer — hardly as good as the Quantum, sigh — from a Brazilian named Grace who told me I need to have babies. She's delivering it to me herself — the Singer, not a baby.

It's the delivery address that could cause a slight problem.

It's delivery day now, and I am leaving class; a lot happened but I've had a problem paying attention, anyway. It's because I'm on a mission. I have a new to-do list (yesterday's was kind of a disaster).

*** Get to Soho. Fast. ***

I have the key to the funky cool dead-plastic-baby GAP-like white apartment where Trucker the Clown lives. I plan to use it. I open the huge gray metal door.

The desk in the room to the left is piled high with papers, but I want to put the new Singer there and pile it high with bolts of fabric. I'm going to beg him to let me. I'm going to do whatever it takes. I also found this guy online named C-T. He had a listing on this buy/sell/find-stuff website for Manhattan. He will bring his van to the post office, pick up my boxes, and take them wherever I say as soon as I make the call.

"You." Trucker's in Calvin Klein jeans with a black T-shirt with the word TEA written in green letters.

"Me." Today I'm wearing a vintage, gathered, Midwest-print 1955 shirtwaist dress from a vintage store called Zachary Smile in the West Village. (I was out of clothes, the store was open late, and Thomas took me down there last night to pick up three perfect pieces in my size.) I'm looking depressed-teenage-housewife sexy. I'm feeling that way, too.

"Now's not really a good time." His face is pale, and I know what alabaster skin means. But I don't have time. I have a speech ready that I spent thirty-five minutes preparing.

So I aim, and I fire: "Please help me. The only place I don't feel surrounded and sad in this city is here in your apartment. I need to feel safe. I'll clown for you. I'll do whatever — well, almost whatever. Can I just stay? And, oh, I really need this room. I need to sew right here in this room. It's urgent." I'm standing next to the piled-high desk. I am not sure why I like the entryway, but it's so great.

The Chelsea was too filled with memories. Even though they were other people's memories. Nina was there last night haunting me. Every time I closed my eyes, I saw her either wearing a bumblebee suit or her black-and-white vintage Versace gown. The one she wore on her D-day. Here in this loft, I shut my eyes, and I see her sewing. She's smiling and wearing a normal pastel blue Jackie O tunic with a matching A-line and nude fishnets. I can picture her the way I need to picture her.

"If you break up with me, I'll kill myself," yells a voice from the back kitchen where I once sat drinking a Sprite. The screech is louder than the fire engines I keep hearing on these city streets.

"Do you want me to call your mother?" Trucker yells all the way back to her. He does not sound happy. Oh, no, he does not sound happy at all.

The siren goes off again: "If you would stop doing that girl who just knocked on your door —"

"I didn't knock, I just came in." *Shouldn't she at least get her facts straight?* "I have the key."

Trucker shushes me.

"— we could get on with our lives!" As she finishes, I stop and take it all in. It's nice to hear fighting that I don't have to partake in. I decide to keep my mouth zipped for the rest of the fireworks.

I hear him say, "Marni, I've known her for two days — and, believe me, it takes longer than that to get into a girl's pants. It took me three to get into yours." Now he is walking back toward her. They fight in the kitchen. Why do people always fight in the room where they keep the knives? I stand in the gallery with the terrorist Jesus painting.

"You *want* to do her, then, and that's just as bad!" She is throwing things, like Cracker Jack boxes, against the cabinets. She's stomping her feet on the ceramic tile floor.

I am not sure how I feel about this conversation, since it is my sex life these strangers are fighting about. Or maybe Trucker met some other girl two days ago. I try to get my heart to stop pounding or else they're certainly going to hear it pop out of my chest.

"Who said anything about sex?" Trucker is raising his voice to his girlfriend — about to be ex? — in the crescendo of their fight. "She's a really cool girl, and she has nothing to do with why we need to take another break. The fact that you follow Mini Kiss all over New York City, Marni, is becoming a problem. And you're drinking nonstop."

"You're just jealous of them! And you're lame because you won't party with me anymore." She's crying in an eerie wacko way. Maybe she has Soap Opera Reenactment Disorder.

"I like champagne." I have no reason why I want to interject. I must need attention.

Trucker shushes me again, his eyes wide and his head shaking a frantic no. Then he turns to her, but he doesn't raise his voice. He's fighting like an adult, something I don't think I've ever seen in my whole seventeen years. "I'm not jealous of them. I think you're becoming obsessed. It's not healthy. And I could put up with it if you hadn't started blowing off our dates, then blowing off the birthday parties we do together, then constantly wanting to go out again."

"Mr. Giggles sucks, Adrian. Face it. The clown SUCKS. I've been telling you this for the last six months." She's wailing while she talks. I'm in a different room, but I imagine she wears a lot of mascara. "Why can't you do something cool like start a band or do improv or go to *Rocky Horror*?" And with that line, she reminds me of my heifer — I mean, mother.

I'm used to fights. Big ones. I wish I didn't get a rush around arguments. I breeze through the rooms of this Soho home as if I pay the mortgage on it. And there she is in front of me, poisoning the air that we all breathe: a girl named Marni who is so pretty she stuns you at first with her eyes, then stuns you again with a mouth so perfect that nothing good could possibly come out of it.

"Mr. Giggles is cool. Leave him the freak alone," I say. I'm not wearing makeup, but if I were, I'd have dark purple sparkle eye shadow on now with thick black eyeliner. I wish I were scary. I imagine in my head that I am five-foot-ten with muscles. Big ones.

"You!" she yells in my face. I recognize her from those laundry detergent commercials. Trucker told me she was the girl who dances in the grass, sniffing fluffy white and yellow towels and saying, "Fresh as the summer day!" I'm surprised I recognize her, as I tend to rent TV shows so I don't have to see the commercials.

"I'm me, yes," I say, clutching my backpack as if it could possibly protect me. I was going for a Japanese manga look when I made it six months ago. I was feeling fierce then, a bit feisty. I tap into my inner action hero, the kind with a superskinny waist, as Marni stabs me with her icy Tide-colored eyes. I notice that she is blond and needs to brush her hair. Her jeans are straight-leg and tight with zippers at the ankles and she wears black flats on her feet. Her top is emerald green, with a collar that slides off her shoulder. Her mascara is superthick and totally dripping down her face.

142

"Um, I know your boyfriend," I say, creeping closer, like a cat planning her attack.

"You probably know a *lot* of girls' boyfriends," she says, wiping at her bright blood-red mega-drama-queen matte lipstick. She's Medusa exploding.

"Take that tone with me again, I dare you." I don't recognize the razors in my voice. They are sharper than I've ever heard them. I scare myself a little, but I don't show it. I feed off of it. I continue to creep toward her, and she inches her body back, back, way back, through the gallery of the apartment, heading toward the foyer office, which is next to the graffiti door. I'm hoping I can steer her right outside onto Greene Street with all the other NYC boyz and girlz. I'm not playing now. I wish I had stared down my mother years ago.

Then she grumbles cuss words with her trembling voice. Her top lip looks like WASP rage manifested. I'm shuddering because she is really buff and she could probably grind me into hamburger. She's like a whole foot taller than me. "Little fashion whore slut. You probably have an STD!" That would be hard because I haven't had actual sex, though things with Muddy were so intense emotionally and physically that I don't consider myself a virgin most of the time.

I'm so in her face, I could slap her down in a second no matter how small I am. Then I think, *This is absurd. Fighting with a stranger over a clown? Acting like a thug? Holly wouldn't do this.* I check out my shoes — twelve-dollar green flip-flops from Ricky's beauty supply store across the street from Zachary Smile. I start to laugh. I mean, I'm threatening someone who stars in commercials while I wear a delicate vintage dress. I need to get it together.

Trucker Hat comes out of the kitchen and into the front foyer where we are standing. "Just tell her nothing's going on," he says to me. There is a pile of pink balloons twisted into poodles on the floor in the living room. His eyes are pleading for help.

So I help him.

"If I'm a slut, your boyfriend is, too. We've christened the entire apartment twelve times, and I hope we christen it twelve more." I am creeping toward him this time like a feline or a Japanimation villain. I turn toward Marni. "TONIGHT."

Trucker covers his mouth, so Marni won't see him reacting. And he *is* reacting. The shock and the pleasure that we're fighting over him is apparent. Before any one of us can figure out what to say or do next, Marni pulls my hair, which isn't even in ponytails today because I borrowed Robert's hair dryer this morning before I checked out of the Chelsea. I feel my follicles being pried loose, like the time I tried to fix the lining of a scooter helmet with Super Glue but stuck my head in before it dried and ripped a wad of hair out.

"Back off, you horrifying creature," I meow into her face. "Don't touch the hair."

"Don't touch my boyfriend!" she screams, then cries. I start to feel bad because her wails aren't normal, they're animal. I don't think she's heartbroken. I think she's got a problem, a real one that has nothing to do with a boy. And, at that moment, I finally *do* get myself together and leave her alone.

"I think what we have here is a misunderstanding," Trucker — Adrian — says.

"You don't understand what *cheating* is?" she screams.

"I actually didn't cheat on you at all. Come on, you know that." He remains calm now, totally done with the female drama in front of him. He's even sitting down on the floor, rubbing the top of his head, making his hair really cute and messy. "I think you're letting Cat get the best of you." His energy seems drained by Medusa . . . and maybe by me, too.

I realize that I have started trouble; I have not minded my own business. These were two of Muddy's biggest complaints about me. Drama and meddling. I am trying to be someone new, and here I am still being me.

I head back into the kitchen to make some coffee to help me cool down. He has an auto-drip maker.

Cool. My family — well, that's me now, I guess — gets some sort of cash for every drip maker sold. Our patent runs out on the hundred-year anniversary in 2008. Then the royalties dry up, too. Supposedly, though, Nina invested in biotech and the fish markets at just the right times, and that should keep me decently clothed.

"Where do you think you're going?" she screams at me. "I want you to get out!" She's picking up the poodles and throwing them at me. But I'm not easily scared by small pink animal balloons. I wonder if he has anything to spike my caffeine with. I'm partial to any kind of hazelnut liqueur.

"She's not leaving, but you are," Adrian says, finally getting a backbone.

"I'll kill myself!" The siren goes off again.

"That's what you say every time we break up. Go directly home, Marni. I'll tell your mom you're on your way." I hear sobbing and yelling from the front of the apartment, then a door slam. They fight outside a while, too. The Mr. Coffee is dripping, so I sit down and look out the kitchen window into a backyard that is the size of a grand ballroom. But New York is weird because there's a square of space out there, a

courtyard between the back of the concrete buildings, and no one has access to it. We can't even get out
there unless we go through the window. I look and
look, and no one has a door leading to the overgrown
wild and beautiful urban landscape. It has a rusty
charcoal grill on it, so someone at some point felt like
I do right now. But not in a long time. I want to go out
there and spark up a T-bone steak. Something moti-
vates me to go to the window and pry it open, despite
the layers of stark white paint keeping it shut. I guess
that it hasn't been opened in decades.

"What are you doing?" Adrian asks, scaring the
liver out of me because I have no idea how long I've
been yanking or how long he's been standing there
watching me. "That's not our courtyard."

"Why isn't it?" I manage to say even though I'm
physically struggling. "Who's going to come after us?
The backyard police?" I'm sweating some more.

"Cat, or whoever you are, I need to talk to you." He
pours himself some coffee, adding a ton of sugar. "Can
you just leave the window alone?"

"I need to go out there right now," I say. "This second." I'm at the opposite end of the apartment from
the front door. My heart gets racy.

"Why?" he asks. "Can you just sit down for a minute?"

"How am I supposed to get that grill to work if I'm sitting down?" I sit down.

"You need to relax," he says, leaning over me to give the window a tug, his arms on each side of my shoulders. "She's gone. You don't need to run away or light things on fire. Okay?"

"Okay." I can smell him, spice and cucumbers. But I remain focused.

I move to the side and let him tug at the window. He doesn't get far, either. I swear I'm going to send a steam iron through that thing if we don't get it unstuck. I turn around and look at him standing so close, in the same room, in the kitchen where the knives are. Before I can think another thought, I freeze against the wall. He walks toward me, and I'm still an ice cube, slowly melting. His lips press against mine in the hottest kiss of my life. This kiss goes on and on and on, and before I have time to get control of my own adrenaline, we have shoved papers and a glass off the steel kitchen table so we can lay on it and make out. Big time. This is my first New York love scene, and I'm wanting it to last as long as it possibly can, from here to eternity. But as hot as it is, I'm not looking to lose my non-virginity virginity at this moment. Maybe not ever. I curse Muddy silently for still being in my head.

My eyes fog up like the windows.

I stand up off the table and straighten my dress. "I've had too much coffee."

"What?" Trucker says, standing back to look at me. He's smiling. "I've wanted to do that from the moment you stole my M&M's."

"How can you make jokes when your girlfriend just tried to ruin my hair?" I ask.

"She's not my girlfriend — anymore." I can't tell if he's happy or sad. He seems in between, like me.

"Oh, yeah." My mind won't turn off.

Where is Muddy now? What is he doing? And with who? Is he lying on a kitchen table with someone else besides me?

"Can you tell me exactly when we did it twelve times in this apartment?" he asks, laughing. "I kind of don't want to miss that."

"Just now?" I say. I'm so confused. This is going somewhere but nowhere. Two busted hearts equal one big fat mess. I didn't come to New York for more messes. "Wait, that wasn't actual christening, of course."

"Do you want to christen it this weekend? Twelve times?"

"That's romantic." My heart is pounding, and I just want a T-bone with garlic butter.

"I'm kidding. I don't want to christen you." He is looking down at his knees.

"You don't?" Now I find myself turning away when I really shouldn't be acting offended.

He stands away and looks at me with his brown eyes. I can almost tell what he's thinking. Almost.

"I'm not — " *ready*, I want to say before he cuts me off.

"You said you wanted to stay here?" Now he's sitting at the table in a steel chair with a perfect view of the unused courtyard. He hasn't bothered cleaning the shards of glass off the floor.

"I'm listening."

"I'm making a judgment call. I think you're only capable of petty crimes. I need to ask you, though, can I trust you?" His cell phone is ringing. He hits silent. Then he picks it up to leave Marni's mom a message. He turns back to me as he sweeps the broken glass off the tile floor. "So, can I? Trust you?"

"You can trust me." I want him to be able to. I just don't want to end up hormones pumping on the table again until this aching inside me goes away. The hormones dull pain for a few seconds, but then I hurt more when they stop raging. A lot more — I mean, I'd rather go outside on Greene Street and let a taxicab run over my right leg than feel emptiness. I feel the emptiness of Nina, of Muddy, of myself. I feel loss, but I don't feel lost. Does that make sense? I want to be the person he can trust. I want to be myself but better. I don't tell him that he's right. Forging one's identity, including one's high school graduation documents, is probably the tiniest of petty crimes.

"You said you'd do anything? You know, in order to stay."

Why do I say things like that? My mouth goes, and my mind gets behind. Then I have to live with my words.

He comes closer, closer, closer. He's not trying to grope or kiss me. But his hand is now on my shoulder, and his fresh coffee breath is near my ear.

I whisper, "I can't go back to the Chelsea tonight. My grandmother is haunting me there." So close to him, my hormones act up again. I pull back.

"That's weird. My grandmother haunts me when I go, too. She wrote poetry while she lived there in the eighties, and I like to say hi to Stanley once in a while. My parents are older; she died when I was little." He's whispering, and I want to know more, but I don't ask. The way his lips move comes out like a poem of its own. I've never seen such sexy red lips on any guy. And he doesn't have on an ounce of clown makeup. "Back to this staying-here thing," he says. "If you really want to, there are four things you can do." He whispers his conditions in my left ear.

I look into his vast brown eyes, and he is not playing, not one bit. How do I get myself into these things? Can I even *do that*? I'm willing myself not to go in for another deadly kiss.

Then there's knocking at the door.

"Don't get it," he says, his breath hot in my ear.

"I have to. It's probably Grace."

As she places my new Singer on the desk just inside the door, I pick up Trucker's phone and call C-T to schedule an ASAP delivery.

This is Chapter Fifteen.

My third-ever class started at nine A.M., and it is currently thirty-nine minutes after. I'm nowhere near FIT
in Chelsea, either. First I took a train to Hoboken, New
Jersey, to withdraw some money. I know I can be
tracked by these withdrawals I have to make, so
I'm trying to throw off my track. I learned that Frank
Sinatra was born there from a man who had a dancing
parrot on his shoulder and was roommates with Weird
Al in college. He also said the zipper was invented
there, and I smile because I love zippers. Then I zip
myself and my cash up to Harlem to meet a guy who
will help me bc me-but-someone-else permanently.
This identity guy Thomas knew, his name is Sal. He's
my man.

Sal and I stand on the southeast corner of One-
hundred-twenty-first Street and Amsterdam, wherever
that is, in front of a bodega that has a large yellow
New York Lotto sign in the window. I hand Sal a white
envelope stuffed with my daily limit — five hundy
fresh out of the ATM.

I don't freak out about how much the new Cat

Zappe driver's license, birth certificate, Social Security card, and high school diploma are costing, especially since I'm no longer paying one-hundred-and-twenty-five dollars a night for the Chelsea Hotel. Trucker does let me stay on Greene Street, as per our agreement. But nothing is free.

I am freaking out about how intensely manically hot Sal is. I'm sweating, and it's not just because the humidity in this city is heavier than the concrete that holds it all in. I see a twenty-year-old guy with *Fight Club* abs who should be in Hollywood or at least on Broadway and not up here promoting illegal activities. The hair is golden. The teeth are white. The biceps are tight. I've never seen such a square jaw and such a great chin dimple on just one guy before. "Hi. So, how are *you*?" I ask and immediately feel stupid, very stupid. Plus, I'm not feeling my black jersey dress, remade to look forties, flirty-fabulous with a V-neck and capped sleeves. It's cute, but I didn't make it. I just haven't had time to sew my stuff in the city. It's too gruesome. And what I make fits me better, and my confidence is all tied up in the fit. I look around me, and the girls are wearing short shorts, jeans — all supertight. I even see gold teeth.

"To the point." Sal isn't looking over his shoulder. He doesn't care if the police witness our transaction. He taps his foot, gives me that *hurry up* look.

"Don't rush me." I'd be able to work my inner attitude junkie if I had the red dress — everyone needs one — that I knocked off from last year's Milly collection.

He starts walking away. This guy is too hot for his own good. He has my money. He still has my papers. I have to follow him. I don't like it.

"Look, you wanna do this?" He wears a gold ring on the middle finger of his left hand. It perfectly matches the color of his skin. *Wow.*

"Whatever," I answer. I will not let him know he's getting the best of me.

He turns around and walks into the bodega. A bald guy behind the bulletproof glass sells Sal a strawberry Yoohoo.

"You want some?" Sal at least acknowledges that I'm sweating not only over him but also because it's really hot. The New York City sidewalks reeked of warm dog pee at eight A.M. I reach for the bottle. "As if," he says to me, taking the bottle back and gulping down his Yoohoo.

"Hmph."

"Look Miss — "

"If you say my name out loud, I swear to God I will find you in your sleep, and those pretty eyelashes you bat at all the girls, they'll be gone. Ever heard of hot wax?" I truly hope I sound tough. Now I am Cat Zappe. But Sal took my real Social Security number, so he did look up my past to authentically alter my future. Now as the real Cat Zappe, I still have the same real birthday, real birth statistics (I was born at six pounds, seven ounces), my real driver's license restrictions. Like, I have to wear my contacts, and if I die, I donate my undamaged body parts. I even have real GED documentation — a diploma from Phoenix Academics Online, transcript, and even an award of excellence.

"Whatever. I'm too busy for this. I have an audition in forty-five minutes. Here." He hands me the envelope.

"Where?"

"I'm a singer and dancer. It's the remake of *The Sound of Music*. They need a Rolf — you know, the guy that sings *'I am sixteen going on seventeen.'*" Emotionless and thuglike before, he breaks into beautiful song. His deep clear voice is as awesome as his chin dimple.

"Are you a spy for the enemy like Rolf was?" I've so seen that movie. Nina loved it almost as much as she loved *Pink Flamingos*. She'd be into this tough guy.

"No time for small talk. Sorry. See ya." He's walking away. He doesn't even turn to look at me when he yells, "If you ever need a job, you have my number. I could use a girl like you."

This is Chapter Sixteen.

"Okay, since all of you want to make a collection, and almost everyone here can sew — who knew? I've never had such a talented and young class!! — I'm officially changing the syllabus. In the past two days, we've covered the basics. Now we're ready to design and sew." Kera Sahn is dressed hipster Japanese today. The hair is overgelled, the tights are tight and striped, and the denim skirt is short with a green boatneck T-shirt belted at the waist. This outfit is killer, totally well made. She looks her age, which is probably twenty-eight instead of thirty-eight. No jingle-jangles here. I notice that the Japanese girls are particularly giddy today in their shiny duchess satin cocktail dresses. They keep speaking Japanese but the only words I understand are Miu Miu.

"Everyone will be entering, in teams of two, the *CosmoGIRL!*/Bloomingdale's contest that I know you know about. Thomas — and I know you know who he is — did an especially great job of recruiting people for my class this year. Looking at the class roster, all thirteen of you are eligible. Now what I need you to do is *win*. Do it for me, promise? I'll help you. I'll really help you. See, I've been adjunct professor here for five years even though my classes have won numerous awards. The Awesome Socks Award, the WPLJ Dress a Ditz Design Competition, the *ElleGirl* dot-com Fashion Week Challenge . . ." Now she's talking to herself and not to us, looking up at the ceiling while she walks around her desk in circles in the front of the room. The rest of us lean forward and for once don't act like we are over everything in the world. The competition looks like it will be fierce before the first sketch is even drawn. This is a group of fashion freaks who were born for this contest. Kera Sahn continues, "They need to make me tenured — a fashion designer needs health insurance, for Christ's sake."

She should not take Imitation's name in vain, but I don't say this. I'm too excited that this is all happening sew fast, sew easy. She passes out the form. With fake diploma in backpack, I can enter and be eligible to win stress-free. I'm even going to apply to FIT as a freshman for whenever they'll take me.

1. Do they have late admission? Yes, I saw it on the
   website.
2. Will Kera Sahn write my recommendation? I

better be sweet. And hope she let's me stay in when she discovers I'm not registered.

3. Why on earth do we have to enter the contest in teams of two?

"I don't believe in contests." The major goth girl, who appears twelve but is probably nineteen for real, pipes up with a gruff voice. She is wearing her trademark fishnet arm warmers that she made out of hose — how very crafty. She looks like a silent movie star with her long loopy black hair and white makeup under rosy cheeks and blood lips. "They contrive rules to encourage world obedience. I'm an anarchist, and I guess you could say it also goes against my religion. Besides, I'd never sell out to a suck-ass store like Bloomingdale's."

"What's your name?" Kera Sahn is about to laugh, and the goth girl looks PO'd.

"Sky Raine is my design name. My real last name is on the class roster; it's Alberta Lipschitz, so you can see why I don't use it often."

"Thank you, Sky. Does anyone else have any objections?"

"I do, because I, like, freak the freak out every time I have to do something that, like, means something.

The world is a canvas that I'm afraid to draw on."The skinny gay guy stands up and raises his arms toward the sky (not that Sky) like he's not afraid of one darn thing and hasn't been ever in his whole entire life. "I just don't perform well under pressure unless it's the right kind of pressure, if you get my drift." He then glances over to the pudgy gay guy who wears a pink skulls-and-cupcakes bandanna with a black skirt and tie-dyed shirt. His name is Dante Heckerling. I caught it earlier when I peeked into his sketchbook. There were some kick-A beauty pageant gowns in there. Not that I'm into beauty pageants.

"What's your name?" Kera asks the skinny guy, who is obsessed with Superfine denim. She is obviously not moved by drama. She doesn't flinch.

"Raisin, wait a second." He pulls a big box of Sun Maids — red packaging with the chick in a red bonnet — out of a tote bag with gun appliqués all over it. "I absolutely cannot live without these, so I don't try. Ask me for some and you're definitely going to get on my bad side. I am not playing. My life revolves around my blood sugar levels, and I get a little dizzy when —"

"Does anyone else have a problem with this contest?" Kera has a kind negotiator face. "Will both of you agree to enter if I ask you nicely as a personal favor to me?" She is starting to draw on the chalkboard. She's writing down a timeline of when we should complete our sketches, first drafts, outfit revisions. We only have a week! Awesome! I love pressure. "Sky, I have a wonderful collection of classic goth fabric at home: metallic serpent embroidered silks, silver fiend jewelry, and lots of other things to inspire you. I'll bring them in if you'll reconsider."

"What do I get?" Opal pipes up, her sapphire about as big as my head. What could a rich girl with credit cards possibly need?

"What about *me*?" Raisin pops out of his seat and says me like *wheee* and makes a big circle with his hand.

"No way," Sky says. Then she starts losing ground, her voice becoming weak. "I just don't want to support Bloomingdale's. You know, I don't believe in commodification. I don't want to support the man."

"Just support the woman, then. This woman?" Kera Sahn points to herself, right in the heart. *Ahhh, how earnest.* "Please. I know Raisin is in."

"How did you know?" He's going through his manbag. He throws a rainbow-striped ribbon necklace around his neck with a small pair of scissors dangling off. He whips out some measuring tape to put in the back of his tight plaid golf pants. (He's not wearing Superfine denim today.)

"Whatever," Sky gives in. "Just let me play my music. Is everyone into Slipknot?" I'm totally scared of what this girl might do to my extremely delicate ears. She's wearing a tiara, but the rhinestones spike up in the shape of devil horns.

"Only when you give me more Tylenol," I say under my breath. I hadn't meant to say it out loud.

"Eat mercury," she says to me, sticking her tongue out, which is, somehow, bright red. Then we look at each other and laugh.

I dig Sky.

163

"Fine, everyone bring in music," Kera says. With that, the whole class sighs collectively. What music do ghetto fab, Asian hipsters, gay coolios, punks, goths, mods, superstraights, and me have in common?

"We okay now?" Kera has long, thick hair weaves that are so cute and long and clean.

"Dude, we're on the edge of our seats, freaking-totally-off-the-walls excited!" Cynthia yells, standing up. She's in a black leopard-print minidress today, definitely

Betsey from the eighties. I agree with her. Let's just *sew* already. I get up and head toward the door — the sewing lab is just across the hall — before Kera Sahn asks me to sit back down.

"Wait, I count fourteen students in this room." This is what Opal has to add to this chaotic conversation. She's wearing all navy blue today. I'm being kind when I call her flight attendant chic. "Hmmmm. Has everyone registered?" She is glaring my way.

How dramatic. I kick my desk, I can't help it, even though it's going to scuff up my Mary Jane.

"Cat has been taken care of." Kera Sahn flips through a grade book. "We have an agreement."

I bite my tongue before I actually say, *What? We do?!*

Kera Sahn is looking at Opal funny, not me. I decide not to whip her — Opal I mean — with the seam guide I bought on the way to class. There were white guys working there with hats and long curls on each side of their heads. I actually see those kinds of guys a lot here in New York City. Anyway, there are a few crucial instruments I must have until I meet C-T to get my prize boxes. You simply can't sew without scissors,

measuring tape, a seam guide, clear ruler, hand nee-
dles, white thread, and a bobkin.

Finally, Kera passes out the contest applications
she's been promising us. We don't need to turn them
in until we turn in our clothes, but she wants us to
keep them safe. I start filling it out.

NAME: Cat Zappe

GRADUATION DATE: hmmm. I reach into my bag
and get my forms. May Fifth of this year. Cool.

ADDRESS: 67 Greene Street, NY, NY 10012

COLLEGE YOU'RE ATTENDING NEXT YEAR: FIT

WHY YOU SHOULD WIN (consider this an essay,
no more than 500 words):

I made my first skirt, a wearable lightweight denim
mini with a pink tulle trim, in the second grade. From
there, I started making shirts and dresses. My priority
then was to be a top-notch seamstress like my grandmother.
But once I mastered the skills of lined, tailored jackets, I
moved on to prom dresses. I made several older girls'
dresses with my Nina during middle school for extra money.
I got the dressmaking down to about two hours, every seam
serged or finished. I got sidetracked during eighth grade

and freshman year with social obligations. But that was okay because instead of sewing so often, I drafted. I learned the advanced elements of design, patternmaking, and draping from books and blogs. Then, sophomore year, I took a hiatus from teenagers, all except for spending time with my ex-boyfriend, who let me make him button-down shirts and pants so I could improve on menswear. Since then, I've worked in a trendy boutique, designing, tailoring, and altering designer clothing for teens (smaller labels like Built by Wendy and Luella Bartley and Sonia Rykiel). The best part about the boutique I ran was that I started carrying my own, my Nina's and mine, vintage-inspired skirts and dresses, called Breakfast. I want to submit the latest Breakfast designs to you.

Opal's eyeing me. I don't like it. Not one bit.

"Mother heifer!" I murmur as quietly as I can, but I know Cynthia hears me. So much for lying low. My bra is itching and I hate this jersey-knit garb I paid one hundred and eight dollars for. I can't control it anymore. Opal's getting it.

Cynthia is kicking my chair — *clunk, clunk, clunk.* She whispers over the start of Kera's lecture. "Behave, dude, jeez."

I shoot a *WTF?* look to Opal while I stick up my middle finger underneath my desk. *Bad me, bad, bad.* I am so not being classy.

Raisin's face is in the shape of a big O. Cynthia is tapping her pencil to her desk in time with kicking me while she drinks tea.

Everyone is watching us while pretending to pay attention to the teacher.

Opal pshaws me and passes a note. It reads: *If you're wondering why I don't like you, it's because you are my biggest competition, according to Thomas. And I've seen your sketchbook, and I hear you made the black and purple dresses. I wouldn't be surprised if those things were actually not yours, but from some grad student or maybe a real designer you're friends with. Not that I believe you're friends with anyone important. I don't know where you came from, but you're not from here. Add that to this: Marni is my cousin. Don't pretend you didn't know, either. You're like a parasite, creepy-crawling into my life when I hadn't even seen you before three days ago. Are you following me? Who are you? Don't think I buy that Southern accent for a second. My theory is that you actually came from hell. Just*

remember that I know everyone — and I do mean
every single teen in this town with any design talent
at all. And I don't know you.

I'll rip you to shreds in this class, then I'll do it
again if you don't leave my cousin's boyfriend alone.
You and me are enemies.

And put your middle finger down, that is so
tacky and last decade.

Not hugz, O

I crumple up her note and toss it on the floor. Everything is weirdly interconnected, just like Nina said it would be. I'm freaking and hiccuping, and I didn't even drink any champagne this morning even though the guy at the Harlem bodega offered me some. Then I sigh. It's time for me to use my expertise. Kera is giving tips about winning contests, and I catch the part about learning everything we can about the judges and even trying to meet them. "Everything in New York City is who you know," she says, unknowingly repeating Opal's note. I can see that Cynthia is scribbling down everything, thank goodness. I have to scribble down what I know to Opal:

I'm not with Mr. Giggles. I am just staying there a few weeks. We have an arrangement that doesn't include our being together. Not like you think. Where I'm from and who I am will never be your business, you monkey. But I feel like I should tell you what I know about Marni as a matter of human dignity and not out of the kindness of my heart. Your cousin, and I'm totally serious when I say this, is losing her mind. I know psychological dysfunction; wackos are the roots of my family tree. I've heard everything about her from Adrian, and I have met her, though I swear I didn't remember seeing you two together at Tiffany's until today. She has Cyclothymia, which is like bipolar lite, and if you help her now, she can be treated. (I looked it up in the DSM-IV-TR.) If you wait, she might really kill herself one of those numerous times she threatens to. She's also experiencing bouts of fetishism by following that band Mini Kiss and being obsessed with them in a sexual way. If she keeps drinking, I don't want to think about what will happen to her. I don't know Marni, not really, and she pulled my hair. But after I saw the Medusa in her eyes, I promised myself I would not be mean to her again. If you really care about her, help her and leave me the heck alone. I have the name of a good shrink if you need it. She's beautiful and imbalanced — Marni, I mean. She'll get worse if people go on forgiving her because she's pretty.

Now, leave me alone, and I'll go easy on you. The dresses and the sketches were all mine. My expert seamstress grandmother didn't help me one bit. Want more proof? I will show you in a sew-off.

Flip yourself the bird for me, and go find a tree, dear, and climb it.

C

We stare each other down all during the lecture. I hate when I get like this, all wrapped up in the warped stuff that shouldn't have much to do with me. But I have been reading *Psychology Today* since I was four, and my mother made me live with schizos and bipolars. Marni needs help whether I like her personally or not. And whether I'm sponging off her ex-boyfriend or not.

After our lecture and our lab — FIT even has industrial serger machines that make awesome inside seams — Opal comes up to me, gives me a dirty look and says, "No truce. See you at the sew-off tonight."

Tonight?!

This is Chapter Seventeen.

"I am a little concerned about our arrangement," to Kera I say after class.

"Why, dear?" She is erasing the chalkboard where she had written our daily affirmation: "It's so hard when I have to, and so easy when I want to," by Annie Gottlier. The scent of her Youth Dew perfume is a little too heavy.

"Because I needed to beg you to register me in the class, but then I was having second thoughts." I was putting off this conversation because while I want to be here, need to be here, I don't want to be officially in the class if it means I have to sign up for The Finished Line in teams. I really do not want to pair with anyone except Nina. Ever. But I need to come to this class every day because it does inspire me. And more than that, it gives me the structure and interaction I desperately need so I don't feel like the runaway fugitive criminal that I currently am. Nina would never approve of my being here in the city without going somewhere legitimate every day. FIT is about as legitimate as it gets.

"I mean, can't I just turn in my ideas on my own?"

"No, because teams have always won this competition. No individuals ever take home the top prize. Proenza Schouler, Rodart, Victor, and Rolf? Two brains are better than one. That's why I require teams, dear. Increases our chances." She hands the eraser over and gestures for me to finish the job. I am flabbergasted. I don't think. I just erase.

I am demolished. This contest, like everything else, isn't what I thought it would be. I thought it was my chance to shine alone.

"I know how things work around here — I grew up in Alphabet City. I know the judges. They take my students' submissions seriously. Teams work brilliantly because one person designs and one person sews, and at your age, it's hard to pull off both." Now she's sitting in her chair, looking through a thick *Vogue* pattern book.

"I can do both." I am erasing this board as hard as I can, chalk dust flying around the room.

"Of course you can, dear. I'm telling you that only teams win this particular competition. There are other great competitions you can enter once you're a freshman in college. I'm telling you that I know the secrets to this city. I also know a thing or two about design. You know, I worked for Marc Jacobs and Tracy Reece. But honestly, the rattiness of the fashion industry just isn't for me. I prefer creating monsters instead of working for them." She's got her legs crossed daintily in her chair.

Ugh. Everything has a secret code in Manhattan. Like even the sidewalks: You cannot, absolutely cannot, look anyone in the eye when walking down the street. If you meet glances with a woman, she'll veer away like you're going to take her Vuitton. If you look at a man, he'll come over and try to lick your face. But what I want to know is, why are there so many rules, and do I really have to follow them?

"So you're in, on one condition." Now she's putting together a binder full of patterns she's made, which we've been studying. Those patterns are pretty good if you're into urban hipster wear — think DKNY for people who DJ at small nightclubs.

"Who says I want to be in?" The board is erased, and I wish there was another productive channel for my frustration. I reach into my backpack and grab my seam ripper, looking for something in the classroom to take apart.

"You want to win?"

"I *will* win."

She rolls her eyes. "They all say that. So if you want my help, if you want to be properly registered, all you have to do is make me a dress like your purple one and put little black flames up each side. Now *that* would be hot." She is looking me in the eye. "But purple isn't my color," she adds. "Maybe do it in black?"

"Then what color would the flames be, so they won't come out cheesy?" I stand close to her now as I answer. *I am not going to use my seam ripper.* I look at her, not showing that a) I hate that she's commodifying *me* right now, as I don't consider myself for sale but for hire, and b) I'm freaking because I don't have time for this. Trucker has me booked solid as soon as I get my boxes. And this contest deadline is in one week! Then there's Opal and her stupid sew-off tonight — wait, that's my own fault.

"You're right. That dress in deep purple is great. But I don't want to see anything made badly like that acid outfit I had on Monday. That monstrosity was made by a student from last semester who I would never let into *this* class. It was just the only thing I had clean. It was a wild weekend." I notice the skin on

Kera's hands is rough. That's what happens when you sew all the time.

"Students make all of your clothes?" It's low of her, but smart. I mean, everyone knows that fashion instructors don't make enough money to buy the designer threads they teach us to dream about.

"Yes. Of course." She's got no problem looking me in the eye when she says this. At least she's not ashamed of herself. "Opal made a Jackie O outfit that was to die for. Maybe I'll wear it this week. Raisin creates lovely denim. Now, please do it by this weekend, and we're all set. And don't look so horrified. It's actually a *favor* to you. You'll see. I'll even make sure to tell my friend in admissions to mark that you've paid even though you surely didn't."

175

I put my seam ripper on her desk as a token. Then I make myself say, "Good-bye, darling," and I book it.

This is Chapter Eighteen.

I must meet C-T outside on the post office stairs on Thirty-fourth Street and Eighth Avenue. There are steps everywhere, and this post office takes up a whole city block — that's really big, like the size of twenty, maybe thirty, American Eagles. I am late for our three P.M. appointment.

Nothing makes me crazier than being late or losing my to-do list.

I get lost, of course, because I'm still a New York City newbie. I needed to head west toward Eighth Avenue, and I thought I was heading that way until I was too far east and had to turn around. I also get lost because my head is gummed up: I have to pair with Cynthia and I don't even know if she's good, and I drank too much coffee when I swore I wasn't going to touch the stuff anymore.

I arrive at five minutes past three, but he's obviously not here. I think of the sewing room in my Greene Street apartment; I've been fixing it up before the boxes arrive. My new Singer — adequate but still not a Quantum, sigh — now presides on top of the newly scrubbed metal desk. I put Johnny Cupcake stickers all over everything. The mess of papers and naked baby doll parts is out of my space now. I stuffed everything in a big closet in the middle of the loft, where Trucker's narcissistic alcoholic dad genius stores five hundred colors of oil paints and more kinds of adhesives than I knew existed. I am reminded of Nina's three sewing rooms. They looked like a Mood fabric store, only two trillion times cooler, no bunny or teddy bear decorations allowed. The first was the fabric room. We had vintage floral patterns organized first by color and second by busy-ness; we had reams of the five basic fabric types — silk, cotton, linen, wool, and worsted — all in our favorite versions; we had a closet filled with vintage clothes that needed to be de- and re-constructed. The second room was dedicated to miscellaneous adornments. Tulle and ribbons and buttons were behind clear plastic shelves and glass doors; thread was in every color Pantone ever imagined; drawing and patternmaking materials were neatly stored in flat metal architect files next to scissors and seam rippers. The third room was for action. We had electric and computerized sewing machines in various stages of various projects. The Quantum was the best, and our Bernina Funlock serger was decent, too. We had a computer where Nina was teaching me CAD (computer-aided design) software, which I'm only okay at. I do better with pencil and paper. Of course, we had two mannequins, the small one like me named Sabrina and the tall one like her named Princess Ann. Rough sketches and color-combination swatches were taped over the walls next to inspiring movie posters and magazine clippings. You couldn't tell, but the paint underneath was yellow.

I couldn't hope to have parlors like I used to, but I made my room on Greene Street as nice as possible for when C-T and I get all my stuff there. I also wanted to sleep in my new sewing room, so Trucker took the air mattress out of his upstairs bedroom where we had been bunking. The sleeping arrangements were Part One of his four-part requirement for me staying there. (It was just sleep.) Anyway, he put the mattress down between my new desk/sewing table and the wall, just three feet from the heavy metal front door with the pink, red, and black graffiti on it. I want to be able to sew whenever I want to — I often wake up in the middle of the night to draw an idea or to just stick material in the machine and get it done.

I also want to be able to leave when I want to. In that loft apartment, Nina still haunts me like she did at the Chelsea. On nights when I catch whiffs of the Chanel Number Five soap she loved, I really think I might be losing it. I just get sad. I want her to see this place — the city, the taxi drivers, Cynthia and Raisin and Dante and Sky, and the Miu Miu girls, the loft. She can't enjoy the big art-adorned white walls in this loft-style GAP-like apartment she would've loved. She can't stare out into the courtyard with the broken grill and plot ways to get the window unstuck. When I get the *spin, spin, spin* feeling, I head onto Greene Street to calm down in the New York City stale, sweet summer air.

I stay away from the coffee in Café Café, where I've seen two stars from that plastic surgery show on fX. Everyone there talks too much because their java is packed with caffeine or maybe even crack. I like mine better from the drip.

I didn't mean to get into that whole project of setting up the sewing room because I can do most of my work at school, but I had to. It is Part Two of the deal I made with Trucker. If I want to stay, I have to start producing. I have a heavy to-do list between now and Saturday:

1. Kick Opal's hindquarters during the sew-off tonight.

2. Make Kera's dress.

3. Create swag for Trucker's weekend clown gig.

4. GET TO WORK ON THE FINISHED LINE SUBMISSIONS.

At least I don't hate Cynthia. She doesn't have marvelous design ideas, which I don't mind. She's agreeing to the three pieces that will win us this contest, thimbles crossed. They are based on a theme we call Spending a Day with Holly. First she goes to breakfast at the Four Seasons in my take of her little black dress (for the contest, I'll make one with flames running up at the hem). Holly spends the day shopping in a two-piece casual houndstooth tunic and A-line skirt in black-and-white houndstooth tweed. Then she Cats around for the night in a superflirty shirtwaist button-down dress in shiny satin material, black and white in an elegant flowery print. I'm lucky that I sew fast — I will want to make several versions and submit only the best.

If C-T makes me wait any longer, I'm going to think of more things I need to do. It's now a quarter past three in the afternoon in front of this massive, small-city-sized Manhattan post office.

Then a man scares me from behind. "That's definitely you. Yep, gotta be." C-T finally arrives, twenty minutes after three. "What can I do you for?"

He knows we're supposed to go inside there, fill out the forms for my boxes, then load them up into his van and out into my new mini sewing room. I'm tapping my vintage Mary Janes. I so desperately need those boxes inside, or I would flip this guy off and walk away. He's kind of a heifer, and I don't see why his services were rated so highly on the Internet.

"Tell you what, you little cutie — "

"Don't call me cute." *Tap. Tap. Tap.*

"Okay babe, let's go. I'll put everything inside my ride and take it where it needs to go. You can go on to your modeling shoot."

"I'm going with you." I would never leave those boxes EVER with a guy like C-T. I hand him two hundred bucks. He was by far the cheapest guy for the job. I went to Williamsburg, Brooklyn, late last night to an ATM. The people there are rich but put a lot of energy into dressing grubster. They didn't even have

181

real bowling shoes, just the kinds you buy at Neiman's.

"C-T will do it on his own for nothing." He eyes me up and down, pausing on my boobs. If I were in any other situation in a town where I wasn't afraid of the pigeons, he'd get an old-fashioned smack from my left hand across his right cheek. He is five feet tall, and that's with rubber lifts on his work boots. His sandy hair is mullet style, he has baby-butt skin, and he's missing a bottom right tooth. He sweats a lot.

This is all Muddy's fault. If I could text him right now, I would definitely tell him that I hate him and he sucks and, just for a little maturity, I would tell him Kenneth the tattoo artist kisses better than he does, too, even if it's not the truth. *He* should be helping me with these boxes.

"What do your initials stand for?" I ask.

"Cow-Tipping Dirty Weasel. It's my street name, one of those things that's a little inside joke. See, I'm really from Indiana, and when I was about twelve —" He's dripping now.

"Okay, enough." I turn toward the post office doors.

"Anyway, my real name is Christopher." He's really small, and I'm worried that he can't pick up a baseball bat, let alone my twenty boxes.

I get out my iZone, and I take a picture of C-T. "I have a record of you now," I say, walking through the United States post office doors. "Don't try anything stupid."

He mumbles something about how C-T ain't never been stupid. We take everything to his vehicle, which turns out to be a tiny old Civic (it was supposed to be a cargo van!), and pack it with so many boxes that there isn't room for me. I try about two hundred different ways to squeeze in, but I can't.

"Sorry, you have to take the subway. See you on Greene Street." He's sniffing his armpit when he says this. "Smells fine," he adds.

I offer to drive and then give him the car back, but he says no way. Then he is gone.

I have no choice but to trust him.

This is Chapter Nineteen.

I called C-T fifty times on Trucker's phone. He finally called back at nine P.M. saying he had to stop in Queens for a sandwich, but he'd be right down.

I

am

a

mess.

I don't care about my old diary, my patterns, my extra pairs of contacts, and my favorite stuffed hippo I can't sleep without. Nina's Givenchy collection is with that slimy heifer. Her amazing diamonds and jewelry are probably being sold online by now. Yes, they're valuable, but I don't care about the money. Those things are all I have left of her. I can hardly breathe, and now I have to leave. If I miss the sew-off with Opal at FIT, then she automatically wins. I want to beat someone tonight. Why not her?

Trucker tells me it will be okay, and he'll wait by the door until I get back.

"It won't take long," I assure him. I am so angry and sad and angry and more sad. But the truth is, for the first time ever, I just don't feel like sewing tonight.

When I open the door to the sewing lab — I asked Kera for the keys — I see Opal and the Chanel-wannabes, plus Raisin, Sky, Dante, the Miu Miu girls, and Cynthia.

"You can do it!" Cynthia uses her pink side pony-tail for a pom-pom.

Raisin's face is in the shape of an O, as usual.

Opal is standing at a table, drawing, getting ahead of me. A large suitcase is next to her, full of her sup-plies. My backpack is filled with a few decent things I found at Mood.

Dante steps forward. "Here are the rules, since I'm a neutral party and think all of y'all are full of too much angst and drama." He's got his own rolling suit-case, and I'm guessing he just wants the extra time in front of the serger. His contest partner, the super-straight Lacoste girl Liz who has no sense of humor, is there sketching.

Sky turns on her thrash music.

Dante scratches his bandanna, his red hair poking out, and adds:

"One: You have three hours. I gotta get out of here

by one so I can get some sleep. Two: Design and sew something cool that a woman can actually wear. Three: Submit it to me at precisely one A.M., and I'll tell you who won."

"I ask you, respectfully, what do you want us to create?" Opal is sharp, razor sharp. I don't care one bit if she's drawing ahead of me. I figure she needs the head start.

"Like something New Yorkers would wear, not Amish people?" Dante says, drawing at the same time. He's wearing tights under his cropped sweatpants. "Liz, can you look at my bustier?"

"I thought advanced students did corsets?" I asked him. Nina taught me those in the seventh grade so I could practice them: all of those pieces and the lace up in the back and the boning! They're super hard, and she said I'd have to do one for sure in college.

"Oh, Cat." Dante waves his head like a magic wand, and all eyes are on him. "Corsets impose their shape on the feminine, or sometimes male, body. Bustiers, glorious bustiers, derive their shape from the human figure."

I nod. I'm impressed, but I'm not going to say so. Obviously, he implies that bustier will be just as difficult (it's still kind of the same as a corset, but I don't want to dance on his good vibes). I just honestly don't know how he gets his grand ideas done because he spends a vast majority of his time outside smoking.

Lacoste Liz coos. I don't understand why; Dante's gay. He's not a queen, but more of a hick-turned-marvelous homosexual. He's kind of a Popeye type. I'm surprised Liz is so into him because I totally assumed she was boring. Just yesterday, she said she didn't believe in booze, mechanical pencils, or R-ratings.

Others are starting to go to their work tables. But not me. I watch how Dante caresses his printed silk fabric. He has passion. Watching him makes me realize everything I have lost today, and I don't feel like sewing. I kind of don't feel like breathing. If I move, I'm afraid I might pass out, or worse, cry. So I stand frozen in the doorway to the lab looking at everyone but not seeing them. It's my conscious blackout. Cynthia comes over to nudge me, tap tapping at my feet with her combat boots.

Around me, the sew-off goes on. Opal asks, "Respectfully, Dante, are you judging?" She isn't looking at me at all. I'm glad because she might take my fragile mood the wrong way. I'm so not fragile over her. It's more like I'm ice; I'm frozen.

"I'll make some calls and see if I can find another non-partisan fashion guru. It will either be me, or me and someone else. Liz, where the hell is my *Vogue*?!" They huddle and giggle over some lace. The Miu Miu girls are speaking Japanese as usual so we never know anything except they're easily excitable. Their sketches indicate that they're working on a line of Gwen Stefani–inspired structured-yet-girly suits.

"Go, go, go," Cynthia whispers to me. I stand in the doorway watching. The clock hands move so slow on the wall. I hear the industrial machines and sergers buzzing. Kids are starting to put together their ideas in cheap muslin fabric which is smart. You always want to see if it works before wasting your expensive beloved fabric.

Opal has finished cutting out a 1940s black evening gown pattern with a supercute Peter Pan collar. That project's not easy, and I don't know how she'll finish in three hours with the gathers and facings. I hear the top of a beer bottle pop off. Raisin is drinking Red Stripe while Liz storms past me. I'm still stuck in the doorway, and it's 10:30. Cynthia has been bugging me the whole time when she could've been cutting out our muslins since I've already cut out our patterns.

"Dude, we can't lose to her! We cannot!" Now she's circling me, actually pulling her crimped strands of long hair. I want to say to her, *We? Who's we?* But that's mean, so I don't.

Cynthia whispers loudly, "She's an uptight, Miss Perfection bitch! It is impossible for someone that rich to have any talent. You act like you know it all, so show us. Show *her*. If you can't show her, how are you going to show anyone else?"

Opal finally does look up from her work to give Cynthia a dirty look, but she doesn't let anyone distract her. Her concentration is like my mother's when she's working. Nina's attentiveness was astounding, too.

I can never concentrate fully. I'm always working something out in my mind — from death to kissing my roommate to losing boxes to placing the buttonholes just right — but it's never kept me from sewing before. I rally myself. I am ready to work this out with Opal right now. "Cynthia, can you find some pinking shears? And, oh, my holy freak, I hate this music."

189

I pull out the purple blended fabric I just bought, shiny and stiff and nice. I also have some silk shantung in black. Kera Sahn is about the same size as me, I figure. So I grab the huge roll of blank pattern paper in the corner, and I pull out a body-length's worth. I drape it flat on the ground, then lie faceup on top of it and make marks all around my body. I make the boobs a little smaller, the hips a little wider. I've done so much fitting and altering that I think I can guess Kera's measurements.

I lay my fabric over my rough pattern. I cut so many pieces. I make the darts, the gathers, the high waist that hides the tummy. I start pinning it all together. I don't need the mannequin yet. I am numb.

"She's amazing," Sky says. "I've never seen someone make a pattern like that."

"Shhh, don't break her concentration, dude," Cynthia says, pinning together muslin fabric pieces for our three designs. I hope she'll sew them together tonight. She seems to be speedy when she rallies, and that isn't so different from me.

Opal ignores it all. I've never seen someone nose-to-the-needle like this. The toughest trait to compete against is determination, and I just hope I haven't lost mine. Her dress is sewn up, and she's just trying to get the neckline to lie flat, which is a beginner problem, if you ask me. She wants to attach the Peter Pan collar perfectly, of course. Liz, Dante, Raisin, Sky, the Miu Miu girls, and Cynthia are watching me watch her. How embarrassing. I go back to my purple gathered dress.

1. I use the serger for the side and back seams so the edges will have that professional finish.

2. I work on the straps and armholes, finishing the edges with shiny black bias tape to save time.

3. I add the zipper, center back.

4. I make sure the purple waistband has enough interfacing to stay nice and stiff, but not too stiff.

5. I cut out small flames in black silk shantung. (I'm a super fast cutter.)

6. I go to the machine to sew the flames exactly where I want them, near the hem, on each side.

7. I finish the dress with an invisible hem stitch.

8. I put it on the form, a mannequin I named Lulu, and I look for problems to fix. Luckily, I don't see anything.

"Holy hot and wet Jamaican," Raisin says, eating out of a red box and swigging his second beer.

"Done. Dante, can I go now?" I have hope that maybe, just maybe, my boxes arrived in Soho.

"It's only twelve-forty-five, Cat. Relax. My second judge won't be here for fifteen minutes. Opal, damn, you've got yourself some competition. Even her inside seams are finished." Dante has had many smoke breaks, and he's stashed away his bustier. He is closely inspecting my dress for flaws.

I love this purple dress. I would love it even more if it had a funky lining, but a girl can only accomplish sew much in sew little time.

"I think I've got some major competition, too," Dante says, circling my dress. "But wait a second." He's suddenly not so into my work, and I don't know why. "Keep going, Opal. You've got ten minutes. You might beat her yet."

"As if!" Cynthia yells, bouncing up and whipping him in the head with her ponytail.

"Go smoke yourself," I say to Dante. He laughs and asks me to try on his bustier tomorrow. I only agree because being agreeable might give me a higher sew-off score.

Opal doesn't finish till five after one, but I couldn't

care less. I'm sitting at the table resting. I hope I can sleep later without the weird dreams.

The door flies open. "What on earth do you people want?!" It's Thomas, and he's in a suit. Black, very crisp, very skinny. "Oh, a sew-off!"

Everyone gathers around the mannequins that wear our creations. Opal's 1940s creation is cute. But it looks just like a Butterick pattern I have at home, number 9826. It's one of my favorites.

"Opal," Dante calls. His bandanna has fallen off, and his braided red hair is in rats. "Your seams inside don't look well-serged."

"Hmph." I am over this. I kind of don't see the point.

Thomas talks on his shiny black cell while he and Dante study our evening gowns and discuss.

"Cat, I worship you. Opal, you're my dear pal. This is not an easy decision." Then he barks into the phone, "I'll be right there, sweety-poo. I know the Lakeside Lounge." He gestures at the rest of us to give him a minute, walks out of the room, and I finally get antsy about winning. It feels good.

He just peeks his head into our sewing lab where

we're all sitting on stools. "Opal, you win!" And off he runs to the Lakeside Lounge.

"Thomas is right," Dante agrees while Raisin raises his Red Stripe in the air. "Opal, congrats."

"As if!" Cynthia screams. Then she hugs me and says she's out because she has to go to bed.

"Do I get a quick acceptance speech? Please? Come on!" Opal is proud of her creation, and it's cute and all, but COME ON. Don't these people know the vintage Butterick catalog? Mine is my exclusive pattern and design. Not a copy! "I would first like to thank my friends." The Chanel-wannabes squeal. I have no idea nor do I care what their names are. "And our lovely Coco Chanel for creating an image for us to aspire to. I could not have accomplished this task without the wonderful apprenticeship I had at TG-17 last summer on Mulberry Street. I want to thank all of my teachers, past and present. I want to congratulate you, too, Cat, on a very impressive effort." Now she's giggling and everyone else is huffing and sighing. She's like menthol in person.

"How original," I say, picking the tiniest bits of lint from the purple dress that will be Kera Sahn's tomorrow. At least I got something off my to-do list tonight.

"Cat, your dress is amazing, and your technique out of this world," Dante says, packing up to leave. "You want to know why you lost?"

"Not really," I say. I dread going home because I don't think my boxes will have arrived. *Spin. Spin. Spin.* I don't feel well. *Get. It. Together.* Now I must get out of this room quick, simply because I don't want to turn on the waterworks or pass out here or on Seventh Avenue.

"Why? Tell, tell!" Raisin jumps around the room belching and then excusing himself for it.

As I leave the room, I hear Dante say, "It's only because that's the exact same dress she wore to class on Monday!" Sigh. It's the same one I showed Thomas the day I met him at Tiffany's. I don't make it home, actually. Instead I go into our regular classroom, and I lie on some clean scrap fabric under Kera Sahn's desk until she wakes me in the morning.

This is Chapter Twenty.

I've already had two coffees from the nice street vendor who listened patiently to my problems before asking me to buy Avon products from his wife.

While I didn't exactly sleep well in my classroom, I *did* put off finding out if my boxes had arrived. It's stupid to put things off, though. Then they just eat away at you longer.

Dante is the first person to file into the classroom. He holds two cups of takeout coffee. He is wearing the same sweatpants and tights as last night. He flashes me the peace sign. "Cat attack! No hard feelings, bro. You're more talented than her, but probably not quite as talented as the Amish — I mean, me." He says this just for pure weirdness when really he's super nice and normal. I call his type wormal. He hands me half of his croissant as I pull his cell phone out of the pink tool bag he keeps filled with sewing essentials.

I call Trucker to tell him I'm okay. He knew I was at a late-night sew-off and all, but maybe he might be worried. It's wee early, like eight-thirty A.M., so of course he doesn't answer because he's sleeping. I leave him a message that I'll be home after class, and we'll get to work on the second part of my agreement with him.

It occurs to me that someone might be concerned about me.

Today is Thursday, and finally we skip lectures altogether and go to the studio. I whisper to Kera that the purple dress she sees on the mannequin form is hers. She tries to hide her reaction, but she beams. And that makes me beam — until she asks me to do a few minor alterations because her boobs are just a little smaller than I had guessed.

Cynthia and I have our three sketches turned into patterns, and we're drafting a few more ideas. We want to make sure everything's better than perfect. We work well together — mainly because she lets me get my way and offers me organic beverages that taste good even if they are sometimes caffeine-free. Her sketches are straight out of the GAP, which is a fine enough store — you just don't want to copy it. She knows she has a lot to learn. Her sewing so far has been good, but it's just on muslin scraps. The one thing I notice is that she is not that fast.

Opal is being a Madeleine as she bosses her

groupie partner around. Sky, who is wearing neon cat contacts today, is watching and listening to them closely. She keeps talking to them as if she cares what they say. At that moment, I realize popularity is the same at FIT as it was in Queensbury. It's not about the kind of person Opal is, though she's effervescent enough with her snarky comments. While Opal is not a beauty pageant candidate like Madeleine, she has the wardrobe of an actress, full of old names like Chanel and new classics like Verrier. I hear her dad is some major art dealer and also the son of a major art dealer. She does know everyone, including Trucker's crazy painter dad plus celebrity art buyers like Natalie Portman plus young fashion designers like Zac Posen. And, supposedly, Opal's ex is some dude in a British band that performed on a late-night comedy show. Anyway, the class is in awe of her, and I don't think this group is awed easily. I don't like her one bit, but her shoes are lovely. They are the ones I've seen on Nina's feet, brand names like Ferragamo, Bottega Veneta, and Jimmy Choo.

The Chanel-wannabes, Miu Miu girls, punks, coolios, mods, superstraights, and preps huddle around her. Even the Eastern European ghetto-fabulous chick named Honor and the extremely bored architect types, Denise and Staffan, give her drawings compliments. They're good, too. She does red-carpet gowns, which is not surprising. But that's got nothing to do with it. It's like they believe that if they stick around her long enough, her wealth and talent will rub off. It won't, just like Madeleine's smaller-scale appeal didn't wear off on me. At least there's me and Cynthia. She says to me now, "That girl needs to take her wardrobe and jump off the Brooklyn Bridge." Cynthia lives in Brooklyn in a brownstone in Crown Heights. She just graduated from some great public high school called Stuyvesant.

I tell her, "She's not as bad as you think."

"She beat you, dude," Cynthia says. Her hair is light blond today. What did she do, stay up all night dyeing? Wacky.

"Opal and I have come to an understanding."

The biggest surprise to me is that this whole competitive class does respect one another. I wouldn't say there are group hugs and support, but it's not everyone stabbing each other in the mannequin. At least not yet. We ask questions: "Does this shirt design need a placket?" "Can I borrow a yard of fusible interfacing?" "Why doesn't anyone do leather tights?" "Who took my fishnet?!"We help one another — well, most of the time. I try to be patient and not cranky.

Like when Kera keeps sending me to fix the tangled machines with tension problems. Twelve times already today. I can't be the only repair girl.

"You pig farmer!" I say to the serger. It has a timing problem that will require a real technician. "Sky, you'll have to find a new machine. And stop eyeing my color stories."

"What's Breakfast?" she asks, snapping her gum.

"You'll see," I say. The day flies by. The group goes to Mood for final fabric selections, but I go to Soho to a little store called Purl Patchwork with the very best vintage collection. This store is amazing. I see each pattern, and I think of a different dress. I could make a dress a day if I really put my mind to it. I could spend decades at this tidy, well-organized store, but it's making me sad.

I can't put it off any longer. I have to go home, or my current home, the apartment on Greene. I wonder if I can will my boxes to have arrived magically. They are marked with codes: stars are my clothes, rainbows are our fabrics and notions, dollar signs are her vintage apparel, and the ones not marked at all are full of jewelry that I never should have put in the U.S. mail. It all just happened so quickly; Muddy and I had to pack so fast.

I open the pink, red, and black striped metal door to the loft. The way my voice echoes when I say hello tells me that no one is home. The place is empty. Way too empty. As empty as I expected. I'm so tired.

I see a note on the kitchen table:

I'm bringing us burgers and fries from this great place called Corner Bistro for dinner. I want to cheer you up . . . because . . . well . . . your boxes never showed. We'll find C-T, try not to break anything. — Adrian

I go out onto Greene Street, slamming the metal door so hard I think I've broken it. *Poor door,* I think, *it's not your fault.*

But I can't breathe, and I'm spinning like I did at Bloomingdale's, and I stand close to Café Café down the street and I yell the following words, "Holy mother of you-know-what!" until my throat hurts, and a hot actor from the plastic surgery TV show tells me to shut the bleep up.

This is Chapter Twenty-one.

Of course, it's taken all my willpower *not* to call Muddy for five whole days when I'm surrounded by everything that reminds me of him — gangster rap posters on construction site barriers, Sierra Club stickers on city bicycles, the sewing machine that's not the one in his Thunderbird. I hurt all over, and I would like to make him hurt with the back of my silk glove. He wouldn't like that very much.

But today of all days, I'm ready to implode, and it's *his* fault my boxes are missing, and I can't think of anyone better to take this mess out on. I decide to look for a pay phone in Chinatown. I choose this neighborhood because it's not too far from Soho, and if anyone bothers to trace the origins of my call, they'd have a heck of a time finding me here. This place is packed, twenty people per sidewalk square. This part of town is a little weird because there are whole ducks, glazed and cooked with eyes in sockets, hanging in windows. For sale, I see fake Louis Vuitton bags from this season and bootleg DVD movies that are still playing in theaters. There are all these stores that sell herbs (not the kind you smoke), and I even check out a basket of dried shark fins going for two hundred and eight dollars a pound.

"Why would anyone pay so much for a fin?" I ask a small woman who follows me around the store and tells me to stop touching.

"Makes delicious, healing soup."

With that, I pick up the nearest pay phone. It smells like burnt metal and sounds like no dial tone. I have to walk in circles for an hour and try eleven phones before I get one that works.

"Hey, you haven't had your cell phone on," Muddy says when he picks up. "I've been trying to find you since this morning."

"You have no idea the misery you caused me yesterday. And I keep getting these flashes of you talking to Madeleine. Why did you do that *at Nina's funeral*, Muddy? How could you?!!!"

There is a long pause between my question and Muddy's answer.

"I have to talk to you, J — "

I scream because I don't want to hear the sound of my name. That's not who I am anymore! I scream because I don't have my boxes, and it's his fault! I scream because I DO NOT WANT TO CRY! I'm really screaming. It's making my throat hurt.

"You need to calm down," he says. "This is more important than your temper tantrum."

"And you insult me, too?" I slam the phone into its hang-up holder. Then I slam it again and once more — superhard — because it feels good. I need some relaxing Chinese tea with shark fins.

"Miss, no, no. Stop that." A middle-aged Chinese woman who has been watching me the whole time says this to me, her hands in her mom-jeans pockets. She's been waiting calmly for the phone. It's the only working one in Chinatown, and it probably doesn't work anymore.

204   I can't help it — I look at her, and I scream again. But I'm not screaming at her, I hope she understands. "I just don't want to hear anything about home! Talk about home makes matters worse! My grandmother is dead! My boyfriend went back to my evil ex-best friend! A guy with a sweating problem took the only stuff that matters to me in the world! This time, I'm really, really, *really* going to die!!!"

"Honey, here." She pulls something out of her pocket, and then she unscrunches it. It is an origami crane — a long-necked bird — folded on brilliant red, shiny, thick paper with gold flecks. "My Japanese friend gave it to me at dim sum today. If you fold one thousand, you will have good luck for the rest of your life. She's way past nine hundred. You need this more than me." She pats my back, and I don't get mad even though I usually want to punch something when someone gets all up in my personal space.

I look at her.

I feel dumb.

"It's okay, honey." She reaches into her purse and pulls out a calling card with big Chinese letters. "Now scoot. I need that phone."

Why did I call him?

He can climb up every tree in the Adirondacks. Much, much worse is the fact that I only have one thing left of hers: the note still stuffed inside my bra that's sweaty and disintegrating because paper isn't supposed to be stored in foundation garments.

This is Chapter Twenty-two.

I throw myself into my work, sewing like mad while Trucker talks. Then he watches *Midnight Cowboy* and *Breakfast at Tiffany's* on his laptop in my workroom. He's keeping me company, but I can't stop concentrating. If I'm concentrating, my head hurts less, and it's impossible for me to cry or spin.

Nina, missing boxes, Muddy.

Nina, missing boxes, Muddy.

Origami crane.

The next day in class, Cynthia and I finish our first piece. The little black dress isn't so little — it's a huge success. Then we post WANTED signs of C-T the box stealer all around Chelsea. We blew up my iZone shot, and it worked; he came out as slick as ever. Ick. I use Trucker's phone to call Betsy the truck driver so she can keep an eye out for him and his Civic on the Interstate. Sky even puts up a want ad of C-T on the Internet — she scanned in my iZone picture of him.

But I can't think about C-T. I have to concentrate on the two-piece casual tunic with skirt and the shirtwaist button-down fluffy dress.

I

have

to

concentrate.

Cynthia and I are going to work all weekend, and
we should be finished in plenty of time to edit.

It's suddenly Friday night, and even though I have
to work, I also promised Trucker I'd go out. So before
I know it, I'm standing in front of a door, tinted black,
surrounded by red paint on concrete walls. There is a
crowd of club kids, like ninety of them, and we're
smack in the middle, which makes me rock back and
forth a little bit, and then start dancing, arms really
going.

"What are you doing?" Trucker tries to get me to
calm down. We've both got our going-out clothes on.
Me in the Betsey-inspired yellow dress I found in
Chelsea — I haven't had a second to actually make
something for myself since I've been doing so much
stuff for the contest. Trucker's in his black jeans and
cowboy shirt, which looks supercute because he's so
very New York City.

"Watch this." I dance the Electric Slide. I wave my
arms in the air again. No club kid wants to stand next

to the girl with totally ancient dance moves, so I'm effectively making decent standing room for us.

"Wow. Thanks," he says to me, finally able to breathe and adjust his shoulders. We are outside of a place called the Cutting Room, some emo skeez bar in Chelsea. There's a Mini Kiss concert about to go on inside. "You okay with the plan?" Trucker asks.

I can't believe I wasted a sewing night on *this* weirdness.

"Remember our agreement?" Trucker nudges me. "Or do you want to go back to the Chelsea Hotel?"

"Yes, master," I say. Then I dance around again, Electric Slide full force, so we have room.

"That's better."

I am on Part Two of four of what Trucker has asked/demanded of me in exchange for an air mattress and sewing studio on Greene Street:

2. Help him with Marni

On Tuesday and Wednesday, the first nights he spent without her, I slept on an air mattress next to his bed because he was lonely. (This was Part One of our agreement.) She usually stayed there with him, and he didn't want to be alone. He cried the first night; I could tell by the way his shoulders quaked under his bedsheets. The second night, he told me that he always knew she was troubled, but he'd thought he could help. I asked him if he was just repeating patterns. And he told me yes, his mom spent her life trying to help his dad. I told him that having dysfunctional roots on our family trees doesn't make us experts in anything. We hugged, and I didn't let him know, but that night, I was the one quaking under my covers.

He wants me to help him help Marni, and Opal is in on this mission, too. And that's why we're here at this concert of midgets.

We get into the Cutting Room, and the little people here are totally normal in their jeans and tight T-shirts. The taller folks are total freaks — and I'm talking about cheap pleather and serious eyeliner. A few guyz and girlz have on Kiss makeup — big black wigs and white foundation with their tongues hanging out. I guess they all eat strawberry lollipops or else their tongues wouldn't be so red.

The band, Mini Kiss, warms up and then leaves the stage to get some water and mingle with fans.

And there they are, next to the stage.

Opal gives me a nod of recognition. She knows

why I'm here and respects it. She looks so out of place in her clean-lined, navy blue mod minidress with white piping. She's got her hair styled in a flip, thick white headband included. She holds Marni back when Marni comes my way full force. She's wearing the shortest, wispiest silver-blue dress with spaghetti straps. It's totally Rodarte. Or maybe it's Calvin Klein. I'm not into lightweight wisps of fabric, and I'm feeling a little angry, but mostly inspired.

"You crazy bitch!" She blindsides me while I scratch my right ponytail. "I knew you were with Adrian. Adrian, why haven't you been answering my calls? What about the birthday party we're supposed to do tomorrow?"

"We are broken up. You told me you hate Mr. Giggles." Trucker points out.

The main member of Mini Kiss, LittleSixx, stands behind me and Trucker. Trucker, aka Adrian, aka Mr. Giggles, made me come so she'd act crazy and everyone would believe him that she needs this intervention. I feel used, even though she definitely needs this help. Trucker's told me the stories. I've seen her in action myself.

The stage security guard has to hold her back, and I have to bite my lip and pin my hands to my sides because I am forbidden to get riled up. I have to be silent and stand here and get her to come after me again. To calm down, I think about a dress design with silk charmeuse. *Or what about chiffon?* Trying to control myself is like crocheting, which I hate. It takes too much patience.

"Come over here so I can pull your hair out one by one," she snarls. "You stole my boyfriend."

"Marni, I've told you, we're not together," Trucker says. And that's the truth. He and I have too much baggage to do anything other than couch-dance right now. Ick. She is less beautiful every time I see her, just like my mother. Trucker doesn't get too close, but I can tell he wants to stroke her hair. It's understandable. I love and hate Muddy, too, and I'm starting to believe the cliché that love and hate really are the exact same thing. A year ago, Trucker and Marni were happy together. She didn't snap until a few months ago when the Tide commercial came out, and the serious acting/model pressure set in.

"Mom!" Marni says as a gorgeous woman who

looks just like her and weighs maybe one hundred pounds extends her arms for a plastic showy hug. She's wearing last season's Rodarte dress, definitely.

"Hi, Aunt Lauren," Opal says. She's sneering at me, but whatever, there's enough drama here that I don't need it from her, too. So what if she beat me with her stupid, admittedly cute vintage (Butterick, I swear to God) dress?

I just can't take keeping my mouth shut. I cannot, so I say: "I'm really sorry I pushed your buttons the other day at Trucker's loft."

"Who's Trucker?" she asks.

"Me," Trucker says.

"That's so stupid," Marni says. "You only wear those hats for tragic irony!"

I roll my eyes. And she hisses at me! Actually hisses. "Hssss, hsss," she goes.

Trucker's friend Bailey shows up, and at the exact wrong moment he says, "Yo, Adrian, let's just go to Lombardi's and eat." Trucker tells him to shush. He heads my way, breathes on me, and I push him away with an *ewww* because he reminds me of Hogzilla's boyfriend Russ. Bailey lopes over to talk to some guy they just graduated with. They went to someplace private called the Little Red School House.

I continue, "I was taking all my rage out on you. I have a bipolar mother who knows she has a problem but never helps herself. It isn't fair. If you don't get help, you're going to end up just like her, high-functioning at work, maybe, but with at least three husbands and a mother you can't stand and a daughter who hates you. You don't have to live that way. Fix it and go out into the world and be whatever you are, but not this."

"Cat, you are so not helping. Not everything is about you." Trucker isn't looking at me when he says this. I hmph and walk toward the bar.

"Honey, we're here for you," Marni's mother says. "But if you don't get help, we can't let you stay with us. You lie to me all the time, and you've been stealing your stepfather's Grey Goose. It's getting pretty bad."

LittleSixx strokes her hair. "Marni, you know we love you, and we appreciate you modeling in our online ads. But we can't use you anymore because you keep not showing up to the shoots, and when you do, all you want to do is go into the closet and drink and —"

"I knew it!"Trucker is so upset. I think about going over to hold his hand, but then Marni will really freak, so I don't.

They all gather round, and I step up to the bar and order a Sprite; I am *so* not in a drinking mood. It's pretty weird to have an intervention before a Mini Kiss concert, but then again, this is New York. I see them in their very serious conversation. Marni and her mom are crying. Then Trucker tells them about the place upstate (my recommendation) where she can take a break from everything that's been bothering her in the city. It so happens that her family has a summerhouse up there, so she can see a shrink on an outpatient basis.

The bartender is totally ogling. So is Sal, who entered the bar five minutes ago. I called him earlier on Trucker's phone.

He's so cute, the identity-thefter who took away my real name and made me Cat Zappe forever. I called him just to see if he got the part in *The Sound of Music*. He said he didn't, but he still has a prospect for me.

"There's a thousand dollars a month for you if you'll run IDs around the city for me. I have auditions all day now. And the French on the Lower East Side want fake work visas so they can wait tables legally. Meanwhile, the Russians uptown want IDs so they can dance at this Bulgarian club called Mehanata on Ludlow. I can't do it anymore. I need my beauty sleep." He's in leather pants and a white wife beater.

"Let me think." I am tempted — who doesn't want easy cash? But then again, I'm already a runaway with lots of fakes. I've pushed the limits enough. "No way."

"What if I get you your own scooter? I have an extra." He's leaning into me, and he smells like Irish Spring. I bet he uses this too-cool-for-you schtick to get all the girls to take off their foundation garments.

"Let me think." While I do miss Nina's Vespa, I say, "No freaking way." And then I push him away even though he smells good, and he's supercute. I even murmur *ewww.* I feel like he's just waiting for the right moment to plunge his tongue down my throat.

"What a waste of time." As he says this, his beautiful face bunches up. "Oh, come on, you know you like me," he says, rubbing my back suggestively. "And I like you, or why else would I come to a Mini Kiss show? I could be at Casimir tonight."

"Get off me," I say. *Note to self: No more flirting with hot actors/thugs.*

"You're not that hot, anyway," he says. Then he knocks the stool over as he heads toward the door, stopping only to give his card to some curvy girl in Enyce.

Meanwhile, the intervention continues over the blast of Mini Kiss music. I try not to listen because interventions give me bad dreams. Like I'm standing in a drive-through at a fast-food restaurant. You speak to a grubby black box, and you have no idea who is on the other side of it, but it's probably someone with festering zits that are going to explode into your spicy chicken sandwich. I would rather bowl naked than trust a drive-through. Or listen to another intervention.

Finally, five minutes later, Opal, Marni, Marni's mom, Bailey, Trucker, and the rest of their entourage walk out of the Cutting Room. I raise my glass to the bartender and say, "Cheers!"

Then Trucker comes back in, throws more money on the bar, and says, "You can't stay in a bar by yourself. You've got a Southern accent, and you're only seventeen."

"I didn't hear that." The bartender runs from us fast, and he checks the next girl's fake ID.

He tries to drag me out by the hand. I say, "Watch my gloves." I hiccup Sprite as we head down Broadway to Soho, back to Greene Street.

"Who was that guy you were talking to?" Trucker's brown eyes are droopy. I think he's tired, or maybe he's sad.

"Not your business."

"And my name isn't Trucker; it's Adrian. Why can't you just call me that?" He's looking up at the black and eerie sky. The night lights in the city make the clouds look like chiffon. I look up, too, which is difficult because I'm also trying to walk.

You're really not supposed to hang out in parks at night in Manhattan, but there's this one called Madison that's pretty on Broadway. During the day, the buildings around it are alabaster. At night, they turn gold from the streetlamps. When it's dark, that's when you can see the gargoyles and steeples. They're shimmering.

Trucker looks really cute. I like when he's feisty. "I totally dig your boots," I say. There's nothing clownish about him at all. We made a pact not to make out. Actually, it was my idea. At the time, I figured that it was really bad to kiss your roommate even if he kisses like a superstar. I told him it was especially really bad to kiss your roommate when your heart's already broken, and you can't offer anything emotionally because emotionally you're dead. At the time, Trucker had suggested that getting physical didn't mean getting emotional. That made me mad, and he apologized, and we've been dancing around each other ever since.

"Can I kiss you?" I ask.

"Nope." He's pushing his golden hair out of his eyes. I reach over to do it for him, and our eyes meet.

I hiccup.

This is Chapter Twenty-three.

We stand there and look up at the blue sky, just lights and gothic statues and no stars. He breaks our two-minute silence by getting in my business. "So tell me, who the hell was that guy?"

"Don't worry. He does fake IDs by day, acting and womanizing by night. He's harmless enough. I mean, he wears flip-flops. Real thugs don't wear flip-flops." I have to sit down. "He knows where we live. Hiccup."

Trucker sighs and sits down in the park on a bench. "Can you just tell me where you're really from? Why you're here? I don't want to hear about your grandfather being some crack addict. And why do you act so angry?"

"I don't believe in acting." Looking up, I have a nice view of the buildings through the branches of oak trees. I can't look too long, though, or everything starts spinning. "Don't go thinking Sprite is my truth serum."

And then, I don't know what gets into me. I tell him I am from Savannah, and I had to come here, to fashion heaven, because my Nina died. Then I start saying everything — way too much about Madeleine and Muddy and Hogzilla and Russ, and then I start going on about how Nina died that night just like she always said she would.

"And that's the absolute truth." I'm leaning on his shoulder. It's soft and warm. Then I scoot back from the sidewalk and lie down in the grass.

"Was she psychic or something?" He listens so intently, and I can see how he would be a good clown. Clowns have a way of reading emotions and reacting to them immediately.

"Nah. She just believed something so strongly that she made it come true." I explain to Trucker that my Nina's time to go was July the seventh of this year. She had this premonition a long time ago, after a day and night of partying with illicit substances and student radicals in the late sixties. She dreamed that's when she would go — peacefully, right in her sleep. And she did on the date I always dreaded.

"I told her how dumb predicting your own death was. And I told her I never wanted to hear about it. But then she'd mention it to me on her birthday every year. Last year she turned seventy, and when we toasted — Perrier-Jouët, of course — at the Sagamore Hotel, she said, 'To our last!' Then she had the nerve to go and smile about it, which I will never understand. It was so sad. Then she told me right there at the bar that I wasn't allowed to cry on her birthday." I lie down on the bench, my head in Trucker's lap. He feels my forehead.

I keep talking, and Trucker keeps listening, and I don't know why I've kept this in for so long. I have never told anyone, not even Muddy, about Nina's D-day. "I said to her, 'Nina, you *are not* leaving me, and I believe *that* strongly enough to make it come true. There is no one else, not my mother, not my dad, not my then-boyfriend, besides you to take care of me.'"

Trucker rubs my hair before I hiccup. Then he takes his hands off me.

"Nina told me that the world would not always be kind, but that I would succeed. That I was not the type of person who would ever be alone. She said she'd take care of me long after she was gone, and you know what? I told her I didn't want her money, I just wanted *her. Eff the drip coffee empire.* Then, that night, she got drunker, and she talked about the things she'd done she was thankful for — like Frank Sinatra, Tommy Hilfiger, *and* Steven Tyler. She told me that she'd screwed up badly when she had a daughter by not ever being around and always chasing men that weren't my grandfather, who died before I was born. But she felt like she'd had the chance to get it right with me, her granddaughter. Then she said the other things she was thankful for, like going to the beach in Maine every year in August. Like making and giving away hundreds and hundreds of pieces of beautiful, handmade clothing. Like making friends absolutely everywhere she went." I stop to breathe and choke back the waterworks.

"I told Nina I loved her and not to leave. We went home that night and watched *Funny Face*. That's the one where Audrey Hepburn plays a bookkeeper in New York who goes to Paris with Fred Astaire. You know, she dances like a freak in a bar?"

"I'll have to download it," Trucker says. He's looking up at the oak branches, too. From his lap, I can see how long his eyelashes are.

Then I think about it, how for all of my junior year, what made me more miserable than anything high school drama could concoct was that I was totally afraid — make that deathly terrified — that July seventh would come and her crazy dream would come true. I'm lying on the bench with tears streaming down my face, and Trucker doesn't touch me. He asks me to go on instead, and my voice isn't even cracking. "That day came. In the morning, I left Nina's house right after we made Nutella crepes. She swore everything was fine, and she felt fine, and she promised me that she wouldn't go out of the house. I was afraid if she did, a semi or something would run her over. She absolutely insisted that I work my four-hour shift at Miss Priss. It was an awful afternoon, and I got into two entanglements with customers. So I returned to her place where everything was still fine, and we started sewing first drafts of a special summer dress we came up with for our Breakfast line. Long story. I left the house at seven-thirty P.M. because she told me to get her a cherry Slush Puppy from Seven-Eleven. I came back in the door at seven forty-five, and Nina was in her favorite Givenchy gown, lying in bed. She was smiling. She was dead.

"She left me three things:

"1. A printout from a stupid website called Death-clock dot-com that also gave that date as her last day. I don't know why she believed in this stuff.

"2. A printout of a study with her writing on it: 'See. And don't ever think this was your fault!' The study was called 'Patients can predict their own demise' and was written by doctors named Poulton and Butdorf from a medical journal called *Critical Care Medicine*. It was about people who believe they are going to die and how they do it suddenly and painlessly. The only reason I told everyone it was a heart attack was so they wouldn't gossip about her. The town, as much as she was loved, had enough to say about my grand-mother already. I ripped that study into tiny little pieces on her bedroom floor.

"3. A note on Kate Spade stationery telling me exactly what to do.

"So I packed the boxes. Instead of storing them at a secure facility that she had already lined up for me, and instead of living with my then-boyfriend's parents like she wanted me to — she did *not* want me living with my mother — I had the boxes sent to New York City. And then I followed suit."

A bunch of clouds roll over the sky, but they just make the buildings and the light more beautiful.

"She was right about one thing, Cat," Trucker says to me as we stand up to head back to the loft with the door covered in pink, red, and black graffiti. "Whatever you believe in most can come true. You and me are proof."

That night, I sleep next to him again. This time, though, it doesn't feel like I'm doing him a favor. It just feels right.

This is Chapter Twenty-four.

Kera Sahn makes us all come in on Saturday. The contest deadline is five days away, and Cynthia and I are the only ones anywhere near done. I have to go around the lab and fix people's problems so they'll actually turn out sort of okay.

And I've got a serious stress headache.

"Sky, do you have any Tylenol?" I yell across the lab that's buzzing with sewing machines and chatter.

She passes me some with her fishnet fingers. Then she gives two tablets to everyone in the class. "Take these, I need to put on my music." And with that, the thrashing begins.

Golly damn.

My poor head.

While others work, Kera talks about the "brutal, backstabbing, catty state of the fashion industry." I'm stuck fixing thread wads because Sky keeps messing up her serger, which wouldn't happen if she'd stop singing — if you can call it singing. Then Kera urges us to go out into the business world and play nice, starting with her classroom.

"This lecture is goofy," I whisper to Sky.

"So idealistic," she says, rolling her eyes.

Our teacher continues: "Think of this space as your idea factory and your fashion commune. I want everyone to share and learn. There is no idea that hasn't been thought of before. Learn to communicate. Start working together today to make the fashion world of tomorrow a better place. And learn to *share*, people." She's all goth today, and I don't think she's into nu-metal. This look doesn't suit her — ripped fishnets, vinyl black Bermuda shorts, and a black polo tee with bloodred arm warmers sticking out of the capped sleeves. Weird, but whatever. I'm sure this is something Sky made for her to wear.

Cynthia is so into Kera's karmic speech that she bounces up from her stool and says, "Group hug!" And they huddle up. Everyone except for me, because it's just too kooky.

Kera ties it all up by writing on the chalkboard, *"Big things are expected of us and nothing big ever came of being small." — Bill Clinton.* Then she adds, "As Tim Gunn would say, 'Carry on!'" She even uses a terrible fake-Brit accent.

While we are in a competition — one that I intend

to win with the help of Cynthia's slow but steady sewing skills — this is nothing like a reality TV show. We really do want to help one another. Even Opal and I made a sort-of truce. This morning, she was waiting by the glass doors out in front of the building.

She had on oversize sunglasses but took them off when she said to me, "Thanks for your help last night."

"Whatever," I answered.

"Really, you *helped* Marni. You've helped people in our class. I don't hate you as much anymore." She followed me while I walked down the FIT hallway toward our class.

"Thanks for the update." I finally turned around just to see what she was wearing. It was cute as usual, a flowy Chanel sundress in peach. She has no idea that labels actually mean nothing unless they are your own.

"My only problem with you now is that I want to win the competition, and you're the person standing in my way. How much could I pay you to just leave?" Opal was so intense, whispering, of course. "I'm an art heiress, you realize. Simply state your price."

"No freaking way. You're not the only girl in New York with access to cash. *I'm a drip heiress*. Now out of my way, snitch, I've got a dress to make today." I could totally believe what she was doing because it sounded like something Madeleine would do. Like when we bought the answers to our geology final from our teacher, Mr. Nathan, in the seventh grade. We saved up my allowance to do it because Madeleine didn't have cash like Opal does. She only had caché, which is almost the same thing.

I laughed at her and took off toward the lab again. "Out of my path, you monkey," I said. "I have a contest to win."

Cynthia saw the whole thing, and later she slipped me a note that said, *Go dude!*

Now she's freaking. "Are you sure we don't need to redo this?" Cynthia asks as we stand over our table, shaking because she had too much vanilla soy latte. I need to slip her a rum and caffeine-free Coke. Her eyes are so wide that she looks like Bambi's mother, and her whites are so white that the gray in them sparkles. She confesses that she's really upset because she's missing her hair appointment with Krister the Swedish stylist in the East Village. She had wanted blue streaks today.

"Oxygen. Breathe it," I suggest to her. Really, she

needs to slow down and take in some air. I suggest she go out on Seventh Avenue for a second, but she acts like she doesn't hear me.

"How do I learn to design?" she asks as she goes back to her sewing machine. Some people are meant to be seamstresses, expert ones, like for the couture houses in Paris. Why can't she just be happy with that?

I interrupt her. "You do something for me," I say, flipping through a book called *High Fashion Sewing Secrets from the World's Best Designers* that Grace at Chelsea Sewing brought to me. It's great for learning better techniques for hidden hems and even buttonholes.

"We could write that book," she says, braiding her crimped hair. "What do you want me to do, Cat? I am *not* breaking the law. My dad's still a Canadian, and he could be deported," she says all hushed and in my ear. "Like, I can't even jaywalk." The other students are buzzing about fashion, and she's buzzing about immigration status.

"I may need you to finish this line for us —" Then I get interrupted before I can explain that I've been having the weird dream about bumblebee suits. That must mean something that's not good.

We fit our second outfit on the mannequin, Princess Ann, and the Lacoste skeez named Liz says, "It's nice."

"I absolutely cannot and will not do any of this without you," Cynthia says. She's tapping me on the shoulder so I'll look her in the eyes even closer. "I need you."

Raisin does real swan jumps at this moment. His right arm pulls him forward with the momentum of the subway as he leaps through the air. He steals the colorful wispy scarf that was draped around Opal's shoulders. He flutters it around the lab. His and Opal's theme is the Red Carpet Goes to the Ballet. Apparently, Opal ditched her Chanel-wannabe partner when she realized Raisin was a serious tailor and designer and businessman — he's already selling his wraparound skirts made from vintage tablecloths in Williamsburg while he saves up for his dream denim fabrics. But still, Opal's skills are *skillz*. She's designed three dresses that will be appropriate not only for starlets but also young people attending events like evening art show openings, movie premieres, and mosh pits. Raisin is killer at sewing them together, and he's a draping genius.

They're good.

We're better.

"But we can't fool around," I whisper to Cynthia, who nods so fast, her head might squirt right off.

Raisin hops my way and Opal's scarf tickles my shoulder. Then the scarf brushes over Cynthia's hands, which are pinning our black-and-white big flowery print silk fabric I found in Soho.

Raisin stops dead in front of Princess Ann and, still in a frozen swan pose, his eyes double in size. I place my body in front of my/our/my work.

"Cat, stop worrying," Cynthia says as she puts antibacterial lotion on the back of her hand where the red scarf had been.

232 "Ohmygoddessinhighheaven!" Raisin yells, leaping, leaping between the machines and table. "I'm not going to steal anything from you. I'm going to worship you. But I'm still going to whup some Breakfast booty."

"Shut up, Raisin, she's got a big enough head already," Opal says, summoning her partner back over to her coven.

"Hmph," I say. What makes me madder than anything is that he knows the name of our line, and he utters it. I know this is stupid, but for him to be so flip is disrespectful to my Nina. Or maybe I worry that my use of the name with another partner is what's disrespectful.

Spin.

Spin.

Buzz.

Kera walks over to me and says, "Oh, stop it — peace, love, and FASHION over there."

"Unclench your fist and put down that middle finger, girlfriend," Raisin sings to me. Then he breaks into opera: "You're scaring me!"

Oops. I mean to be classy. I don't get my problem. I don't get *me*.

With this, the Miu Miu girls whose names I finally caught, KeKe and Lee, run over to Cynthia and me. They're having a serious conversation in Japanese. (I know a few words — I've seen both *Kill Bill* movies a few times with Nina.) All I can think is, *Good lordie almighty, I need to get it together.* I choose to blame Sky's music.

"Everyone, come look at this!" Kera says, motioning the class to our work. Cynthia puffs up like a stuffed guppy and all of a sudden she doesn't even look petite. She does a cartwheel. I roll my eyes; I don't want attention now. I only want attention when we win. Kera adds, "Wow. You all better get to work or else consider the competition a wrap."

"Like a Fields and Feta Wrap? The one from," Raisin breaks into song, "Awww Bon Pan that you can eat?" Of course he knows how to pronounce it. He does more ballerina jumps and Kera asks him to settle down while Dante tells him to relax. Dante's awesome, and he works in the corner quietly with Liz. They are doing a line Dante calls "Marie Antoinette, if she had access to technology." Everything revolves around a bustier, one of the most tedious and difficult pieces of clothing to make. His first entry is a black suit with big turquoise dots and a bustier underneath. Second, he does a bustier with jeans, romantic but modern with silver and plastic turquoise embellishments. Third is the bustier top toned-down ball gown. It's deadly. But he doesn't put up with attention except from Liz, who is obviously in love with him. Anytime he gets her eye, he slips outside for a smoke.

"Cat, can you please explain your work? Then we will go around the tables and talk about what else needs to get done before submitting on Wednesday." Kera wants to make me a guinea pig for an inspirational group share that I'm not in the mood for.

"No." I huff.

Cynthia takes over, and I want to thump her head like a ripe melon.

I give her eyes that say, *We are not supposed to talk unless we win.*

She ignores me. "Our theme is *Breakfast at Tiffany's* meets the Lower East Side."

"Where's the Lower East Side again?" I shuffle our sketches into one stack so at least my classmates can't copy *everything*. They'll be able to tell from my drawings that we've made a lot of trial runs of these outfits. That's something Nina taught me — make your masterpieces in muslin not just once but many times, and perfect them later. "Is that near Chinatown?" My crumpled origami lucky crane is sitting on my sewing desk back at Trucker's apartment.

"Think sixties class meets CBGB's before that place lost its lease." Cynthia speaks a mile a minute. "Think Sex Pistols meets Givenchy. Think Bloomingdale's meets Yellow Rat Bastard. We're not doing *cliché*

Audrey. We're doing a What Would Holly Wear Today line. W-W-H-W?" She reaches for her Fiji bottled water.

"The Sex Pistols had a really cool name, but let's get honest, they sucked," I say. "They were all stylized hype." Dante nods.

"No, it's much more simple than all of that," I continue. "It's just Holly Golightly gone modern! Sheesh. Now leave me — I mean us — alone. We have one more whole outfit to get done." Everyone else has more to do than that, but still, it's not my problem if they are behind.

"It's hot," Raisin says as he walks around the room, his red scarf flowing behind him. He asks for advice on how a sleeve should be finished on a gown made for the Oscars. Sky and her superstraight partner, Scott, want a hand with their line of infantwear — she's doing children's goth clothes — and I tell her I'll help if she will stop bringing in music. Svetlana and another goth named Tracey ask for a new idea for their painted-on stretch jeans line they call 2Cute. Then my head starts spinning, and I walk right out the door of that classroom. I march down a long hallway and down two flights of steps and out the glass doors that are propped open because the air-conditioning isn't working. I stop at the Sabrett's hot dog stand and talk to the man hovering inside a cloud of juicy, smoky steam.

"What is wrong with me?" I ask the hot dog man.

"You're too intense. You're too focused. You need to try something else." Then he tells me my dog is on him. "Avon makes great lip gloss. Want to place an order?"

This is Chapter Twenty-five.

"Have you ever seen that movie with Madonna in it? The one where this housewife gets mistaken for a drifter in New York and mayhem ensues? You totally remind me of that movie." Trucker is Mr. Giggles today. He's wearing a fuzzy red afro and a big white suit with red polka dots. His red patent leather shoes are size twenty. He is setting up his balloon-tying station before the children arrive in ten minutes.

"*Desperately Seeking Susan?*" I say. I'm in a black-and-white striped T-shirt with a boatneck and skinny black pants. I have one ponytail high on the back of my head. It's Part Three of our agreement — I have to be a clown assistant. I chose this outfit from an old movie called *La Strada* where a girl gets sold to a trouba-dour, basically to be his slave. Not only is he making me clown around, I also had to produce these little toys for him to give away as presents (swag) to his four-year-old audience. Trucker wants to make a good impression on these kids' parents because they pay at least a thousand dollars for his one-hour performance.

I am all about self-promotion and self-employment and teen career-building. I don't mind making giveaways — we put Mr. Giggles plus his web address on the toy tags. I found a free stuffed animal pattern called Pointy Kitty online — I haven't made stuffed animal crafts since second grade so I needed a template. I made fifteen of these six-inch animals with Grace's help. (I had to hire her to finish them up, which I don't tell Trucker. I only had time to make half of the Pointy Kitties, and I had to get at least five hours of sleep!) "Madonna plays a prostitute in that movie. What kind of girl do you think I am?!" I yell this, and some Soho House manager comes over and tells me it's an expensive members-only club, and I had better act like I belong. I stick up my middle finger, and Trucker quickly reaches for my hand puts it down, apologizing for me. I tell him to watch it, or I'll throw out the Mr. Giggles press packets I made up for him.

"Actually, you remind me more of the housewife character, Rosanna Arquette, who gets mistaken for Susan all over town and really loves it."

Suddenly, it's showtime. Trucker says, "Mr. Giggles says hihellohowareyou?" and dances and juggles

Pointy Kitties. He hands our swag to gleeful preschoolers. "Hihellohowareyou today? Hihellohowareyou? I say!" His song is cute. His voice is deep but friendly. They look at him, admiring and giggling.

This is what he and his dad fought most about, he told me last night while we watched *Funny Face*. His dad thinks he needs to be a serious artist, like in the Met, and not a laughable one. But Trucker not only graduated in the top five at the Little Red School House last year, he's also been scholarshipped into NYU's acting program, which *never* happens. That's because he had so many recommendations from satisfied customers. People who hire him dig him. So do children, who keep asking for hugs. I mean, it's a little embarrassing. He wears a wig often. He's always practicing new magic tricks, making new animal balloons like the monkeys he's perfecting, and he's really into all the stage makeup. I can see why his dad and Marni weren't supportive. They just weren't open-minded enough. Actually, this party is why Trucker's dad flushed his car keys down the toilet. He told Trucker that the word *clown* comes from the words meaning *clot* or *clod*. He was superembarrassed that his son was starting to get gigs at Soho House, where major art dealers hang out. Mr. Trucker, his dad, thinks that splashing terrorist Jesus on canvas is high art.

Wait. Aren't artists supposed to be accepting?

I'm accepting.

I hate judgments.

I know what it's like to not have people approve of what you love. My shrink mother heifer always told me that fashion stood for all that was evil and commercial in the world. "You are contributing to your own demise — you deserve the heartache you'll find in your chosen field," she'd say as we ate the macaroni that Russ made for us. I was good in all my subjects at school, including math, and I would remind her that my career possibilities were infinite, as I was only sixteen at the time. She went on to remind me that Madeleine Baker actually received higher marks than me. Okay, so I was tenth in the class at Queensbury High, and she was fifth. *So what?* I want to be Jill Stuart plus Betsey Johnson plus Marc Jacobs all in one girl. Trucker wants to be the new Captain Kangaroo.

Trucker delights the kids with these yellow monkey balloons and Pointy Kitty toys. After his tricks, songs, and juggling, we get up and do a dance to *Bob the Builder*, which happens to be Trucker's favorite show on PBS Kids. He calls me his Wendy, since Wendy's the one who keeps Bob organized and gives him creative new ideas.

After the show, we go into the Soho House library to try to sneak a drink from a bartender there. The green chandeliers are made of Swarovski crystals. The light is clean, low, and romantic. The leather seats we're sitting on make our couch dance all the more comfy.

"Salut!" he says, inching close to me.

"Cheers!" I can't drink too much. I have to finish my last design if it kills me tonight. Our submissions are due Wednesday, and we need Sunday through Tuesday for revisions. Cynthia will be at the loft by eight. Trucker is going out with Bailey. He says we're too intense when we work, and we stress him out.

We get through a whole glass each of Perrier-Jouët. We inch closer during some sexy, slow music.

"You really are great, and I don't want you to believe anything anyone else says about Mr. Giggles," I say to him, my head down because if I look up, his eyes will be right there, even with mine, and who knows what will happen?

He reaches for my chin, and he looks me in the

eyes. His breath is so sweet, and it's also minty because he must've snuck in a green Tic Tac when I wasn't looking. He kisses me on the leather couch.

And kisses me.

And kisses me more.

I'm tingling and spinning. It feels like eating the best chocolate you've ever imagined, like imported milk chocolate from Switzerland. It's indulgent and luscious and sexy, but still sweet. As I kiss him, I'm not even thinking of Muddy or my missing boxes or my lost Nina. I'm only thinking about me.

This

feels

so

incredibly

good

and indulgent

and luscious

and sexy

and sweet.

"Hey, I will not have clowns making out on my couch. I won't have it." The bartender's tsk-tsking us and tapping me on the shoulder.

"Back off or I'm going to tell you how badly your

pants were tailored!" I yell at him, adjusting my striped T-shirt.

"I'm just saying, you love weirdos, that if you want to have clown sex, you're going to have to rent the Playroom." He's inspecting his pants, and they're hemmed way too short, just like I said!

"What Playroom?" I ask, smoothing back my black hair that desperately needs more dye.

"That's what they call rooms here. It's like, what, six hundred a night?" Trucker says, way too knowingly for me. "What?" he asks, looking at my frowning face. "We had our walls painted at the loft, and I stayed here. Shame on you. I'm not that kind of rat. So, what do you say, Cat?"

"You two just can't keep kissing here. The young professionals who come in the evenings will think we've gone high school. Oh, the horror!" The bartender marches off, his shiny black pants flit-flitting as the legs brush together.

"We don't need a room. We just need to cut it out." Now the moment, hot as it is, is lost. I am happy when I'm with him. And I'm sad when I think about all that I've lost.

This is Chapter Twenty-six.

It's really weird living with a guy I'm starting to care about. He and I made a pact after the time on the kitchen table to take it slow. I made him promise that he'd be gentle, not grope me, and make sure any smooth moves were initiated by me. I mean, not to put him down, but he's a guy, and I know how guys are when it comes to testosterone. I wanted to play this friend-ship-roommate-whatever-we-are situation safely.

He said that would be fine, and that's how it's been for the last five days. The problem is, I can't take any-thing slow. We kissed all night after the Soho House clown show, whenever Cynthia was or wasn't look-ing. He didn't even go out with his friend Bailey to some club called Bread. He claimed he wanted to work on MrGiggles.com while Cynthia and I sewed. But I think he just wanted kisses. Who doesn't? They were more innocent this time. They were sweet and not frantic. They were intelligent — like kissing between long lines of dialogue.

Cynthia didn't complain. I got the feeling she dug it, which was weird, but I'm not going to think about that right now. Despite the many distractions, we finished the dress at two A.M. with just a few details left to iron out. After a huge discussion about how badly we want to win, we need to win, we *will* win The Finished Line, we all crashed in my sewing room. I didn't even want to run out the pink, red, and black graffiti-striped door.

I took two iZone photos of them. One of Trucker, little white specks of makeup peeking from his earlobe. Then one of Cynthia, who finally did get the blue stripes in her hair. I put the photos with the note from my Nina. (I *had* to take it out of my bra. It's now in my backpack.)

I looked at it for a long time while I tried to fall asleep. I know I can win because I have no Plan B right now. But Opal and Raisin aren't my — I mean *our* — only serious competition. What about the bustiers? I'm superstressed over Dante and Liz's modern, technological Marie Antoinette. It rocks.

The weekend was bliss, but as is often the case, Monday comes.

"Rip it up at class," Trucker tells me. He has a nice body. I'm watching it and ignoring his lame jokes. We have walked from Greene Street to FIT. He needs to buy clown supplies in the garment district. I'm going to help him with some new costumes. I want him to look like a more modern and sophisticated clown, especially if he wants to keep working at Soho House, where the women wear nothing less than Diane Von Furstenberg.

We turn left onto Twenty-seventh Street from Seventh Avenue, and that's when I see *it* sitting right in front of the entrance doors to the Marvin Feldman Center.

I stop. I stare. I gasp for breath. Trucker grabs my hand to keep me steady because I'm wobbling on my Mary Janes — and not even because my feet hurt.

"This cannot be possible," I say to Nina and myself and to no one and everyone in New York City. "Why is everything so complicated?"

"You know, you probably just need some more comfortable shoes for all the walking you do," Trucker says to me as he looks in the window of a warm-smelling bakery. I think he's going in for a crumpet, but I don't look. I can't look.

I'm staring at the mint-green 1969 Thunderbird in disbelief. The engine is running.

Get. It. Together.

See, this is the part where I would like to spin and see bumblebee outfits. I could pass out and flip out and make a big scene on Twenty-seventh Street. But instead, I start thinking about the Misfits, and how they were badasses, goofy punk pioneer rock stars who loved quirky songs like "Teenagers from Mars." *I'm a badass,* I tell myself. Then I think about Holly, who would've stood up straight — I adjust my posture — and remained calm and cool in a confrontation. *I'm poised,* I tell myself. But then reality sets in. What is happening cannot be thought away.

I go dead inside.

My past is in front of me — Nina, Hogzilla, my missing memories, everything I've lost.

"What do you want, Muddy?" I ask, adding to myself, *I'm a badass. I'm poised. I can handle this. I'm a New Yorker now.*

"I'd like to have my laptop back, for starters." Muddy is tanned and smiling. His biceps are so defined, and I am not ready to see him. His hands are beat-up, telling me he's been hard at work, too. I knew this would happen, that we would meet again. This was in my dream. I just thought I could get through this contest first. I need to finish The Finished Line. It's my goal and my everything.

"Listen, darling, can we, like, do this another day?" I say trying to sound breezy. "I'm free next Monday. How's that?" Breakfast is due Wednesday, winners are announced Thursday, Friday's the last day of class. "I just don't see why this can't wait." I don't want to feel dead today. I have to *design*. My past just kills me. As Holly would say, "This is too gruesome."

Muddy rolls his eyes at me. Then our pupils meet. And meet. And we're staring each other down just like old times. As usual, I win. He looks at the ground and he says, "Fine. But I can't promise I'll know where your boxes are by then. What? Don't look so sad. Come here."

I step toward him because he is my magnet. I do not want to see him, so I have no clue why we're hugging. But when we do, I'm no longer dead inside. It hurts, but I'm feeling. "You found them for me?"

"You knew I would." He's nuzzling his face into my hair. My hair is becoming damp.

"I guess I did." Muddy has a way of fixing things. I step back from our embrace, and I try to get it together.

Crying might be the healthiest reaction, better than spinning or screaming, but I'm not going to do that right now. I'm just not. "Did you bring my Singer Quantum?"

"It's in the trunk, where it has been since you last bruised me." He leans back against his car and folds his arms. He is not as emotional as I am. Or if he is, he controls it so much better.

I punch him in the shoulder. Hard. We are standing close. He leans in to kiss me, his soft, familiar, hello-I-miss-you peck on the lips.

I stop him.

"What the flip? You and me broke up. You left me here in New York City to rot."

Trucker steps in, crumpet bag in hand. I don't know how much he's heard, but he's definitely heard something. "Cat, you're hardly decomposing," he says. His eyes tell me he wants an introduction, but I'm not giving it.

Muddy laughs. "Cat, huh? Is that what you call yourself now?" Then he leans over to my new room-mate and says, "That's pretty good. Pretty clever."

"You were paying attention?" I say to him. At least I'm looking nice today in a vintage black dress with white polka-dots I found at Zachary's Smile. It's got the perfect skillfully gathered and pin-tucked bodice. But the best part is this: If you look superclosely at the dots, some of them show a tiny pink bird breaking out, like breaking an eggshell, and joyously flying away.

"I paid attention to everything, and that's exactly why I needed the break." He leans over to Trucker. "I'm Muddy, by the way."

"I'm Adrian."

They do not shake hands. They just nod, tough-boy-style. Both of them fold their arms across their chests.

Muddy isn't one to beat around any bush. He looks at me as he says to Trucker, "So that was fast. Are you her new bitch? Because I'm her old one."

"How dare you come back here and insult me and my friend. Give me my machine, leave it right here on the sidewalk, and go home." I turn my back on him, and I hold Trucker's hand. I'm only doing it to get on Muddy's nerves. Trucker must be reading my mind because he lets go. Then I turn around. "Well, except I need you to bring me my boxes first. You know I do."

"So . . . at least this one isn't middle-aged." He's leaning forward now, stepping away from his car and toward me on the sidewalk.

"Kenneth was only twenty-one." I stomp my foot. Then I feel kind of stupid.

"Or maybe he's your teacher here at FIT?" Muddy says, squinting his gorgeous green eyes.

"*Shut up.* What have you been doing with Madeleine since I've been gone? Tell me *that*. Like I even wanted you to find me," I say, moving away. Trucker has moved even farther back.

"You didn't make it very difficult. When I arrived yesterday at three, I had a plan: First, I'd check for you at Tiffany's. Second, I'd look for you by the Milly collection at Bloomingdale's you always talked about. Third, I'd nose around at FIT. But I found you at number one. I went to Tiffany's and asked every single salesguy if they knew you — starting with the diamond floor, of course. It didn't take long. Most of the salespeople there are women, and I knew you wouldn't bother talking to them." Muddy is smirking, quite proud of himself.

"Thomas." Now I'm slouching, and I'm not feeling like a badass or like I'm poised. I'm feeling transparent, even with this dress.

"He said I'd find you here bright and early. You are in some class, trying to win a Bloomingdale's contest."

Muddy now goes back to his car and leans on it, dares me to walk his way. "That one you've been talking about for the last two years."

He had been listening. But I always knew that. I do move toward him, ever so slightly, despite myself. "Where did you stay?" I ask.

"I found a cheap room at the Sheraton in Weehawken, New Jersey, right above a Houlihan's where I could go and *flirt with chicks.*" He winks at me. "Actually, I looked out the window at the view of Manhattan last night, and I pictured you in the tallest building."

"What would Madeleine think about that?" I'm sneering at him, and he's smiling. He's just trying to get to me.

He goes on. "Maybe you should call her and tell her — what's your name again? Cat? You know I don't like the city. The only reason I ever considered coming here was for you."

I go to his trunk and start heaving my heavy Singer out of it. It feels like it weighs six hundred pounds. I have to set it down on the sidewalk despite every intention to take it into class and somehow get it to Greene Street.

I want to spend forever and never with him. Muddy, I mean.

"You're not going to class today. You're coming with me," Muddy says. Trucker's not very tall anymore. He stands at least ten feet away, next to a sculpture of a crocodile eating some money.

"No freaking way." I really can't pick up the Singer again, even though I'm trying. This is not a portable machine. Neither of the guys offers to help. They're watching and waiting to see what I'll do next.

"Your mother has your boxes," Muddy tells me. "When you called, I hunted her down, and I barged into her house. In case you care, she's moved into Nina's house. Your stuff's stacked up neatly in one of your workrooms. Your mom cussed me out bigtime — Russ had to pull her off me." He is now putting my machine back in his car, and I'm not protesting. My heart drops. This is all about Hogzilla. It's always about Hogzilla. She is seriously going to ruin my life. Again.

Trucker goes to the trunk, and he rubs the handle of my sewing machine's carrying case. "So you two have been talking —"

I'm really stomping my left foot now. I can't hit Muddy and certainly not Trucker. I don't know what else to do. I hate my feral pig of a mother, and I want to hurt her. Or at least burn every piece of clothing she's ever worn. While she wears it.

"Your mother is the talk of Queensbury, New York," Muddy says.

"I *knew* you weren't from Savannah!" Trucker goes back to the crocodile sculpture. "I *knew* I shouldn't have trusted you."

"I bet she's told you a lot of things, haven't you, *Cat*? I just love saying your new fake name. *Cat*." I'm glad Muddy can find humor in this. I smack the side of his shoulder, but he stops my hand.

"We've always been too physical, don't you think? No hitting unless you have your gloves on." He's laughing. I smack his arm again but it doesn't make me feel better.

"Get in. Let's get your stuff back."

"I'm not going anywhere with you. Ever." We're standing off again. Staring, staring, staring each other down.

"Stop with the drama. You don't have to put on a

255

show for Adrian. He's already in love with you, look at him." Muddy is getting comfortable in his convertible at this point.

I go to hug Trucker, but he won't let me touch him. He won't even let me touch his gorgeous hair. So I lean in. "This isn't what you think. I just have to go and tell off my mother. I'll be back."

"Apparently, nothing is what I thought it was," Trucker says, arms folded, his off switch on.

"But I'll be back." I hug him while he stands there, still and stiff and not hugging back. "Please try to understand. You've got to try to forgive me for what I'm about to do."

"My question is," he starts, not meeting my eyes, "are you a phony? Or are you a real phony?" He's still looking at the ground, and I can tell he's sad.

That's one of my favorite lines from *Breakfast at Tiffany's.* I touch his shoulders on both sides and I say, "I promise you I'm the real phony."

I go to the car.

Muddy takes me where I'm not ready to go.

Part 3
LIKE YOU DIDN'T KNOW I'D HAVE TO GO BACK HOME . . .

This is Chapter Twenty-seven.

I will not spin. Maybe. I will not resort to physical aggressiveness. Definitely. I will not curse. Unless I have to.

I *will* get what I came for.

My to-do list is supershort at this moment:

1. Take possession of my boxes.
2. Get back to NYC in time to fix our submissions and turn them in!!!
3. Don't cry.

As we pull in, Russ is in front of the eight-bedroom Victorian that Nina and I kept spotless. Ick. He needs to wax or put his shirt on. He is weeding the impatiens—purple and white—that line the walkway. My stomach flips to see him near them, let alone touching them. Nina and her hot gardener planted those high-maintenance flowers themselves. I watered them every day even when I didn't stay the night.

They look the same. At least they haven't shriveled up and died.

She can take care of the impatiens, but she could never deal with me.

"Hi." I do not like the way Russ stares at me. I *know* I need to pin the bodice so I have less cleavage. Guys like him remind me to do it.

Muddy says to him, "Don't even." He's walking behind me, and we're totally in step.

We walk in the yellow front door of the house. She is standing one room past the foyer, in the dining area. Behind her is the kitchen with the orange vinyl and chrome dinette set. Off to the left is *the room*.

"What are you doing, you monkey?" I say first, standing under the Tiffany glass chandelier. I head to the room, the one that was for the actual sewing. There they are, my twenty boxes stacked high. My clippings are still taped all over the wall. Nina's have been taken down. I am so freaking overwhelmed with happiness because now I feel like I haven't completely failed my Nina. And in some way, I have kept her alive. Now I will keep her with me. I'm jumping up and down, I'm so happy. I'm even hugging Muddy, who seems thrilled, too. I grab his cell from his back pocket and make a quick call while he tells me I have to get a new phone. Seeing my material things all stacked up neatly makes my emotional mess seem less messy. I sort of, for the first time, think I might be okay.

"Don't let your mother see that you're happy," Muddy whispers into my ear. His breath prickles my skin down to my toes.

I turn around, and there she is — Ariel, my mother. She has been watching, assaulting me with those judgmental eyes. "In order to not give you the satisfaction of a huge fight," I say — my posture is never good around her — "I'm going to count to ten. One."

I am so ready to rip her silk blouse off. Who wears a silk blouse with a collar, anyway? The boxes would be better off lost than in her possession. One of the most important instructions from Nina was not to let my mom have her most cherished stuff. She would've died to see this.

"Two," I say.

"Please don't be overdramatic. The boxes are fine." Her hair is just like Nina's. Her tall, thin body, too. But they are nothing alike. Nina would never look so dry and boring. She would never wear a blouse with pleated pants. She would never take anything that mattered away from me. Ariel takes everything.

"Three. What the hell were you thinking?! Four! Five! Six! Wait, just forget this!" I run at her and tell her the truth; that I really do loathe her.

She fishes around in her purse and hands me a bottle. "Here, dear, you need a Xanax."

"Only if you take one, too." This is new. We've tried a lot of things, self-help books, group sessions at the Pilgrim Psych Center, but never prescription drugs. Her heels click to the kitchen. I hear the water running. She brings one glass for us to share.

She takes her pill. I take a sip of water.

"Changed my mind," I say, dropping it on the floor.

She's not happy; but she won't say it. Instead she surprises me by starting with, "You did the right thing by sending Marni up to me. She's progressing nicely. She spends her days at the Sagamore Hotel getting spa treatments and comes to me one hour a day. And just in time. That girl was on her way."

"Thanks, but you shouldn't have taken my boxes, you farm animal. I need them, and I will leave," I say. I really need to stop calling my mother swine names. She's an older Marni in perpetual recovery. It's just that while I understand that she's given me as much as she was capable of, and while I understand that she'll regret the state of our relationship for the rest of her life, I can't help but remember that she's just been so mean. For example, she took that wading pool away from me. She put it out on bulk waste day on a July day when I was four, right after I'd started asking if I could swim in it with Toby. I had gotten to the point where I didn't even need Nina to hold my hand when I got in anymore. I loved it; of course she tossed it out.

I stand here scratching my head — I made time early this morning to do my hair today in a June Carter flip. Muddy has gone to the backyard, and I smell our outdoor grill. He always did that. He likes to make food while the rest of us fight. If we can't get along, the least we can do is eat hot dogs.

"Don't you want to know how I got them?" she asks. She goes to the front door, leaning outside to ask Russ to come in and make us lemonade. Lemonade? Like we're all-American or something?

I follow her. "You probably had me stalked. Or maybe you used Nina's money to hire a private investigator to find me. What did you do with your old house?"

"Don't flatter yourself. I have no interest in

stalking you. But do call Greg in Pittsburgh. Your father heard about Nina's death and your running away and he has been worried sick about you. I haven't been. I knew where you went. You think I didn't listen all of those years? You think I didn't know about your superficial contest? I also knew you'd be back." She sits down at the orange kitchen dinette. Russ puts two lemonades on the table. I peek in the refrigerator, and it is still fully stocked with Nina's Perrier-Jouët. It was the only food we *always* kept in the house. She wanted to be ready for a party at any time.

My mother goes on to explain that when she dropped me at the psych center, she came to this house and wasn't surprised to see that all the jewelry, clothes, and sewing materials were gone. She knew I'd find a way to leave the psych center, too. She just wanted to make an effort to stop me, or at least slow me down.

"Do you really want to know how I found you?" she says, a fake smile on her face.

"Not really." I'm lying; I totally do.

She tells me she went to the most popular online website for selling and buying things and contacted every listing for a Man with a Van in Manhattan. They were all lying in wait for me. Then she paid C-T in the four digits to thwart my delivery — bringing it up here when he said he was having a hamburger in Queens. She adds that "C-T is borderline autistic, and moving things is a good career for someone like him."

"I have no idea why you hate me." I want to raise my voice, but my better self tells me to stay cool. Not to hit anything. Not to feel angry. Or anything else. Well, I do feel a bit of empathy. I mean, my mother had to steal her daughter's most prized possessions in order to get me to talk to her. It's sad.

"Are you going to fix the bodice on that dress? Way too much cleavage. And while you're here, can you put this button back on my red blouse?" She's scratching her long pointer finger over and over.

"I have never hated you as much as you hate me," I lean in to her and say.

"I love you, dear. I always have." She's still smoothing her skin and nails.

And that's when it hits me. This is love to her. It always was. Being critical, in her world, is showing someone that you care. Dropping your kid off at the psych center is taking care of her, not abandoning her. This is so warped, but it's true. It really was the best she could do.

"But here's the deal," she says evenly between sips of lemonade. "Stay with me. Finish high school here, or I'll find everyone you know in New York City and tell them you're a dropout. This is for your own good. I took the boxes because it was the only way to get you here."

"You monkey," I say.

"Don't call your mother a monkey," Russ interjects as he starts a pot of coffee.

"Sorry, that is wrong of me." I pat her hand. I am sorry. For everything because someone here has to be the bigger person, and I'm the only one who's capable.

"I have never had any interest in Givenchy or Chanel or Pucci. And I know how much those vintage clothes are worth. I know how much the diamond necklaces and bracelets appraise for. You think I have any interest in your boxes and boxes of material? Please, all of that is pure commodity. I don't want it," Hogzilla says, but she's not looking at me. "I wanted to get an M.D. and not have a baby. But Nina said she'd keep me comfortable all my life if I had you and just

265

let her raise you. So see, that's what happened. That's why you're here."

"Nina bought me from you?"

"She wasn't perfect, you know," my mother says. "She was wildly overcompensating for her own guilt. While I know I am mildly bipolar, I also know that I wouldn't have disassociated from every person around me if she hadn't been tramping around New York State with everyone but my father, throwing parties and letting me raise myself. She knew she screwed up with me. With you, she tried to break the cycle. She tried to give you enough love for both of us. And you turned out sort of okay, all things considered."

"Why on earth do you think it's necessary for me to know this?" I ask. Just when I think she can't shock me, she shocks me.

"It's just time for us to lay it out on the table. And this is my table now and not Nina's. You and me? We don't like each other. Just because I gave birth to you doesn't mean we'll have complementary personalities." She sighs, gets up, and washes her hands. "But I'm the adult, and I have to take full responsibility for our relationship. You don't want your mother to die without coming to an understanding with her. Believe me, I know. It just happened to me." Russ comes over to hold her hand, but she just washes it again.

I'm squeezing my knees under the table. I so want out of here. I wonder what Trucker is doing. I hope his dad hasn't stopped by or called him. I hope he finally tied that monkey balloon just right. I hope he doesn't hate me.

"I know you get your money soon, in December. Then there's never a reason for us to talk again. Or we can try to fix it. July to December? We have four and a half months. We need to try."

I feel bad for her, but she's had seventeen years to fix this mess, and I'm up for fixing it. But on my terms. Her stealing my stuff is not my terms.

267

"I have to ask the difficult question now: Are you just after the money Nina left me?" I feel awful asking this, but I can't keep tiptoeing around this issue.

"I can see it now, the court hearing of the decade: the battle of the drip coffee machine heiresses," she says. How she can laugh or find anything remotely funny right now is beyond me. "Nina left me more than enough to leave you alone. She didn't want us battling each other. And you know that I don't care about superficial things." She says this as she sits in Nina's million-dollar house, mind you.

I'm starting to get distracted now. I remind myself: *The Finished Line. Trucker and Cynthia and Dante and even stupid Opal.*

"So you'll stay." My mother says this; she isn't asking. "It is just for a few months, and if we don't, we will live with the guilt that we never really tried." She looks down at her hands, and there's still no emotion.

I don't answer. We eat our hot dogs.

I'm dying inside. Yet I'm totally alive. I'm seeing stripes of fire-colored flames dancing around in my head. I am feeling pain in my chest colder and heavier than a freezer filled with ice. I knew Nina was a bad mother, but I never deserved to be a consolation prize or a therapy device. She could've seen a shrink herself or bought a book if she felt badly for neglecting her own daughter.

But instead it comes to this.

I'm put in a place where I have to be thankful — totally thankful — that Nina did the messed-up thing that she did. If she didn't, I wouldn't be here. This is too messed up.

"Want another dog?" Muddy walks in with a second plateful. He just cooked a value pack.

I go to the sewing room, and he follows me. We close the door, and we are alone. He whispers he'll come with me if I want him to.

This is Chapter Twenty-eight.

"Please get the blue Vespa in the back," I say to Betsy from Zap Trucks, who arrived an hour after I called her from Muddy's cell phone. She's between deliveries on her day off. She is picking up my stuff and taking me to New York City for only the price of the gas, which is actually quite a bit in a semi. But no amount would be too much.

My note from Nina told me that above all of her other advice, I had to follow my dream and do what *I* believe. I believe in New York City and fashion contests and the friends I've almost made there. If Nina wanted me to try to work it out with my mother, then she didn't understand that my mother is not capable and never will be. To stay here would be to repeat the cycle all over again, not break it.

Ariel can relate to Marni, but not to me. She can even help and love those people. But not me. I'm just not messed up enough. The truth is sharp. Maybe I don't have to be so angry anymore because I finally realize that. Adults make mistakes, too. Big ones, and they don't necessarily know wrong from right.

But the thing is, I *do*.

I have to love Nina. Mistakes and all — she's all I had. But obviously she was terribly wrong. I'm not going to be angry about her losing the will to live anymore. Though I always wish she would've talked to a doctor instead of just me. She did the best she could, and I just have to go out and do even better.

She was far from perfect but I still love her perfectly.

Betsy, with muscles like a bulldog, carries box after box from the sewing room to her truck. Muddy and I help. We are making a ton of noise, and I know exactly what's going to happen next. Ariel will have something psychological to add.

"I tried, dear. But I knew you'd leave," my mother 271 says from underneath the Tiffany chandelier in the foyer where Nina used to greet her guests.

"You still have me," Russ says, now wearing a Hawaiian shirt.

My mom is aggressively blocking Betsy, whose hands are full. Betsy calmly puts the box down, gets in her face, and says, "I don't think you'd win in a fight."

Ariel moves quickly. "Dear, take this." She hands me the bottle of Xanax. "You need it. When you passed out at Nina's funeral, you were having an anxiety attack. If you ever start to spin, that's what's happening. They're scary, but they're not dangerous. Get enough sleep and exercise. It will go away when you find what you're looking for."

"Thanks." I take the bottle, thinking this is all she has to give to me.

I wait till Muddy and Betsy are in the truck, and I ask her, "Would you know why I've been dreaming about bumblebees? They wake me up. Nina wears bee costumes. When I see them in my mind, I think I'm going to die." Russ shakes his head and walks to the living room, where he'll be for the rest of the night on the couch.

"How am I supposed to know? You're allergic to bees. You're supposed to stay away from them," Ariel says, and she gives me a stiff hug that's awkward and unnatural for both of us.

I pull back and straighten up my hair. "I would like for you to get to know me," I offer. "But you're going to have to come to Manhattan to do it."

This is Chapter Twenty-nine.

I convince Betsy to stop at Cool Beans coffee shop on our way out of Queensbury. She's making a bunch of calls on her phone, anyway.

Muddy and I need to talk. But we need to do it quickly. He's acting funny. I'm acting funny. I don't have time to process us. I can't even think because I'm a nervous wreck to get home — I mean to New York City — I mean, home. I have to help Cynthia do that last piece one more time. I never consider anything finished without at least one revision. It's now eight P.M. on a Monday night!

Wait, he can't run away with me without any stuff.

I order Betsy a hazelnut iced coffee with no milk because that's my favorite. Muddy takes me to the table in the back where we drink our caffeine.

"So," I say, standing up, "this is uncomfortable. What is up with us?" I don't want to admit how much I've been thinking about the clown.

"I love you, whatever-your-name-is-or-will-be, and I

always have." He's sitting, pulling me down to his lap. He smells like gas grill hot dogs, and it sounds gross, but it's totally not. This is Muddy. He always smells like the outdoors. "But I can't come to New York City with you until I tell you what happened with me and Madeleine."

My heart stops.

"WHAT?!" I move to the seat next to him. No way am I sitting on his lap.

"There's nothing going on. Relax." He pulls me back over to his lap, and I resist him. I'm not moving anywhere. "She and I have been talking on the phone and stuff, that's all."

"I would rather you run over my chest with a riding lawn mower, the blades freshly sharpened." I turn my back to him and seethe.

"What a mess," he says, joking. Then he tells me that Madeleine has been asking about me. She wants to make up. She wants to call me. She just wants to make sure I'm okay since my Nina died. I tell him to tell her hi. I don't say what I'm thinking: that she can drop head-first off a flagpole. I don't say what I'm *really* thinking: that she only wants to use me because she'd love to come to New York City, and that she's just playing with his emotions to get closer to him.

She will do anything to be with Muddy. It's understandable. Most girls would.

"I want to be with you, Junebug." He leans in to kiss me. His chest is warm against mine. His arms are strong. His lips are soft. But when we touch, I might as well be touching the table. I feel nothing, so I stop. And that's when it hits me. Trucker makes me tingle all over.

"Can you call your dad to pick you up here?" I'm going to cry because he's my best friend. "I'm sorry. I don't think I'm in love with you anymore."

"Of course you aren't — I left you on the interstate," he says, kissing my cheek. He looks me in the eye. "Maybe one day, Baby Jane Junebug Melitta, I can make you forget all the stuff that's happened here."

275

To Nina, I was always her Baby Jane. To everyone else, I was just Junebug, the childhood name my dad branded me with. To me, I have become someone else.

"There's only Cat," I tell him, prying loose from Muddy, which is hard. "Good-bye." I walk away.

Not until I get in the truck do I cry. Really cry. For the breakup. For Nina. For everything that I am not anymore. For everything I will miss.

"Honey, I'm sorry," Betsy says, hugging me hard so I'll know it's okay to let go.

We truck down the road to New York City blasting Bon Jovi all the way. I sing along to "Bad Medicine," and I start to feel better.

I'm going home.

This is Chapter Thirty.

Even if I didn't get everything unpacked until two
A.M., I'm back. I'm in New York. I can breathe. Wait —
maybe not until Cynthia and I finish dress number
three. We met out front FIT at seven-thirty A.M. to get
an early start. I'm guessing we won't leave the studio
until the second we turn in our work tomorrow at
noon. We have so much to do.

"I'm telling you, we have to make it again," I say as
I hand her a cup of coffee from the vendor.

"Dude, we already made it once, and the others
are great. We made them three times each." She's wearing a bright pink Battenberg minidress by Betsey
Johnson. She says it gives her inspiration. I'm wearing
my favorite shirtdress that Nina made for me, in blue-
and-yellow mattress ticking. It feels so awesome to
have our stuff.

We go to the lockers where our three entries are
stored. She can't remember the combination to the
lock, though.

"Cynthia, chill out and open it." I never knew the

numbers, but there is no way I would have forgotten them.

We open our locker finally by kicking it several times.

And our stuff just isn't there.

It's gone. Disappeared.

"Sorry, girls," Dante says, strolling in wearing a tie-dyed skirt. "Opal's stuff is gone, too. Thank the Amish, mine is here. Someone ransacked the lockers. *I* kept my stuff at home, thank god, or I would be *freeeeaking*. Wait till you see Raisin today." Dante trusts no one.

I reach into my backpack, pull out a pen, and say, "Okay, here's what we're going to do."

I start scribbling down, in order, what needs to take place. And by my calculations, we can finish by tomorrow at noon.

1. Mood for fabric.

2. Notions at P&S.

3. I remember the patterns. I'll redo them while Cynthia runs errands.

4. Cut patterns.

5. Cut fabric.

6. Sew.

7. Sew.

8. Sew.

9. Do trims and finishes.

10. Try not to burn ourselves with the irons.

11. Done.

"Wait — we did other versions. Let's just use those! That will totally work!" Cynthia shouts.

"No way," I say. "Those are not good enough."

She sighs. She has ripped her long, colorful hair from the hair elastic, and it's a mess everywhere.

"This will be our final revision."

Apparently, Opal and Raisin, oddly the only other pair affected by this fishy theft, found out even earlier than we did. They are rushing around re-collecting their materials, too.

Kera Sahn is already there, as well, after an early frantic call from Raisin. She is fuming. She has written on the chalkboard:

"Anytime you have somebody doing positive stuff and just doing their time and minding their own business, people will sit up there and lie." — Suge Knight.

She's ready to backhand someone. But I feel really

good. She is wearing my dress today. The flames up the sides are the perfect additions. The fit is great. The fabric drapes just right. I'm glad she digs the purple even though she usually prefers black.

"Love it," she whispers to me. "Keep your chin up."

"This is nothing," I say as I roll out the drafting paper and lay down on it and make marks around my body. For my Breakfast line, I'm still doing a little black dress, but with little flames up the side, a houndstooth tunic and A-line skirt, and a superfly shirtwaist button-down dress in shiny satin with a big black-and-white-flower print.

I finally have my iPod and my speakers, so I turn up my music, and I'm so psyched — if a tad freaked — to win this contest. Getting a big order and turning it around in twenty-four hours is something I did at Miss Priss. I can do this. I can do this. And I had wanted to do all of our pieces one more time, anyway.

Cynthia comes back, tears streaming down her face.

Raisin is also crying, and Opal is more like me, but with less sense of humor and more curse words. I make lists for them too so they can stop spinning and start sewing.

Meanwhile, Dante's bustier outfits are hot. Liz tells me so.

Sky and her partner's goth infantwear is hot, too, but it doesn't stand a chance. This is a line that's supposed to be sold in the store. Bloomingdale's can't touch it. Sky would be better marketing her work to Hot Topic.

The 2Cute Jeans are hot. But also nothing that Bloomingdale's would sell. Maybe BeBe.

The day wears on. The hours pass like seconds. I'm in super psyched mode because I'm being tested.

Everyone's into the soundtracks from indie movies that I keep on my iPod. I'm an amateur DJ, and with any luck tomorrow, I'll be a professional designer.

My hands are so rough from all the sewing, and they're burned from ironing, too. I often have to stop and help Opal get her pin tucks and gathers right for her Red Carpet Goes to the Ballet Collection. Raisin just keeps drinking Red Bull and wailing, "This is tragic!"

"Stop helping her!" Cynthia screams at me.

Everyone is so edgy today. Even the people whose entries are close to done.

It's midnight. Then it's two A.M. We should be exhausted. We should be collapsing. But at a certain point in the night, something happens to us. We come together. Even the people who are done stick around to help. Dante gives up his smoke breaks to help Opal sew. Raisin steps down from his Drama Queen throne and kneels on the ground to help me hem. Cynthia and I don't even need to talk to each other anymore; we know what needs to be done and we're doing it.

It's four A.M. Then it's six A.M. Opal finishes up and moves right over to our table. She threads her needle with my black thread and keeps going. I take a break and look over her collection, to make sure everything's in place. At this point in the night — morning, really — it's amazing I can still tell the difference between blue and red.

"Don't drift off now," Raisin tells me. "We're almost there!"

It's seven A.M. Then it's seven-thirty.

"We're done," I say. There, in front of us, are the full collections. It's astonishing to me that these clothes — these dresses and shirts and tunics and bustiers — were all just pieces of fabric half a day ago. I feel like a writer who's just finished a novel, or a composer who's just finished an opera. Only our creations are even more impressive — because you can wear them.

There's no time to celebrate. We march proudly to the FIT office and drop off our finished work. On the way back, I see Sky (who, truth be told, wasn't nearly as helpful as the rest of the crew) struggling to get her locker shut. I see a piece of fabric poking out and just about lose it. Her locker won't close because the lost versions of our Breakfast dresses are stuffed in with Opal's and Raisin's Ballet Red.

I walk over, and I slap her right in the face, old-movie style.

She has in vampire fangs today and flits them at me.

"I told Kera Sahn I didn't believe in commodification. I don't like Bloomingdale's. I don't believe in supporting the man. To pander to the big companies is to have your soul sucked out by beasts." She's not even feeling guilty. She's standing tall and proud.

"So why did you only destroy mine and Opal's? How could you do that, you Slipknot bitch?" I am too tired to control myself.

"Number one: Cat, you're okay. But I hate Audrey Hepburn. Number two: I really hate Opal. Number three: Dante's great, but it's more movie set, and it's never going to win. Plus, he's letting me borrow the bustier dress for the Buffy Ball on Saturday night. Number four: You two are the only ones with a chance in hell to win. And you'd just be helping Bloomingdale's get richer. Number five: I didn't dream you'd ever remake them in time. Number six: I don't care if you tell Kera Sahn or not because I didn't turn in my infant wear, anyway. Hot Topic has agreed to carry it, and the designs are already being made in the factory." She laughs loudly while my jaw drops.

"I thought you didn't believe in commodifaction!" I say. I reach into her bag, and I grab her bottle of Tylenol.

Just when I'm about to throw it at her, she walks away.

This is Chapter Thirty-one.

"You think it will be us?" Cynthia asks me as we go to the Comfort Diner to get some good macaroni and cheese, the first real meal we've had in twenty-four hours. I am so shocked that I can't even tell her what Sky did. I'm going to keep it a secret because we rallied, and we did it.

Cynthia and I did the very best job we could.

Opal and Raisin did, too.

We did it together, side by side, and we turned it in.

I don't see any reason to get all negative again. Maybe I'll tell them after we find out who wins. But for now, we've already reached the finished line.

Thomas is the one who takes me back to Bloomingdale's. We go way before the store closes, before the contest gets going, because we want to try on everything in our sizes at least once. I'm excited, not worried, but I tell him we have to enter through the weird subway entrance and not through the one on Lexington Avenue.

I get inside, and I go straight to the third floor.

"Taste. That's what you've got. And cash, I presume. Not just any young girl goes straight to the third floor on Fifty-ninth Street." He drops me off up there, and once he can see I am fine — no anxiety attacks today — he goes back downstairs to the men's department to look for markdowns on Ben Sherman.

They have a section in this flagship Bloomingdale's store for major designers, and I am standing in front of Philosophy di Alberta Ferreti.

"What do you want, miss?" says a snotty salesgirl, and I dig her. Snotty in this setting is the only way to be.

"Size four in that." I point to a black cocktail dress, one that Nina would wear. It's one very much like the vintage Givenchy she put on when she lay down and died. This is my tribute to her. I slip the new one over my head — without the snotty girl's help — and I look in the mirror. Everything that's old is new, after all.

In my reflection, there she is. It's her. And I don't feel quite so alone even though I still am. Trucker hasn't gotten back to me yet. Not once. I stay in that dressing room for a whole hour, screw the snotty salesgirl, until Thomas comes for me. I treasure the time to think.

"Nice, Cat. Now come see if I can pull off a surfer look." He's racing away in his scuffed-up bowling shoes, real ones. "Shame that cute boy you were hanging out with isn't here to see."

"It is." I take off the clothes and put on my Holly dress, just like the one I turned in for the contest, only this one is in pink. In the end, I scrapped mod colors and I made three dresses, this one in pink, one in red, and one in black. Just like the graffiti on Trucker's door that used to make me so sad. I miss him. Very much.

The Finished Line displays are done. I see busy bodies set them up — cool white, nameless, and faceless plastic models from Bloomingdale's mannequin closet are about to strut our stuff. Instead of a real fashion show, they're doing displays of our work. If I want models and a catwalk, I have to enter the college students' contest, which I so totally will one day. Meanwhile, more busy bodies put up the microphones. I hear that one-hundred-and-fifty New York City–area incoming college freshmen competed in the *CosmoGIRL!*/Bloomingdale's The Finished Line this year. Ten collections made the cut, all getting gift certificates to this department store.

Cynthia runs in, jumps up and down, and screams. Our dresses are right on the edge of the collections, where everyone can see them. We are in the top ten. A lot of the kids who've arrived are disappointed because they didn't make the cut. Our labels inside say Breakfast. That, more than any winner or runner-up, makes me excited.

Sal joins our group, and since he's Thomas's friend, I don't stomp on his toes. He gives me icky looks, and I make myself not curse at him. He mouths to me, "If you ever need a job, just call." And I don't care how cute he is, or if he's a star one day, he's gross. Still, every girl and boy around us at least pauses to check him out.

Kera Sahn talks to Thomas, and she is frantic. But she looks good. She's wearing a Coco Chanel knock-off by Opal that's perfect for our dressy event. Kera always wears the outfits we made her when she has meetings with designers or buyers or store owners. What she's actually doing, while getting free clothes, is talking up our clothes to get us internships and even entry-level jobs.

We hug.

I feel so happy.

Susan Schulz is the editor-in-chief of my favorite

magazine, *CosmoGIRL!*, and she welcomes and congratulates us all, and I think in a different lifetime, she and I would be best friends. She's the kind of person you want to share lip gloss secrets with.There's a spiel about the importance of giving designers head starts in this amazingly cutthroat and competitive business.

I whisper to Thomas, "Fashion is not cutthroat. It's so much easier than living upstate." I think the fashion industry is definitely going to suit me.

Then disaster strikes

I don't notice it at first. Someone whispers to a judge, who whispers to another judge, who whispers to Susan Schulz.

"One moment," she says. More whispering.

One of the judges looks at a clipboard, scans the audience, and locks eyes with Kera.

Suddenly, my heart goes *uh-oh*.

An intern is sent to get her. The judges talk to her.

She looks in my direction.

Now my mind and stomach chime in. *UH-OH*.

Kera walks over to me, and says, "I have a simple question. I won't even ask your real name. All I need to know at this point is whether you've graduated high school."

Here it is — the moment of truth. And I can't lie.

"Not yet," I say. "I have two more classes to finish."
Sal shoots me a dirty look. But I want to get real, and not rely on a totally fake identity.

Kera nods once, then heads back to the judges. I can see them make a change.

Cynthia, at my side, looks as stunned as I feel.

"*Who are you?*" she asks.

But before I can answer — and I *do* want to answer — Susan Schulz begins to announce the winner. Looking a little stunned herself, she says, "We have a new top prize recipient because the original one, it turns out, has not fulfilled the requirement of finishing high school. We had to disqualify the wonderful Breakfast collection by Cat and Cynthia, but we hope they'll enter again next year."

She then starts to list the revised fourth place winner, and the third place winner. Once she's said the second place winner, we're all extra nervous. Opal and Raisin haven't been called yet.

And then she gets to first place, and their names are called.

It's instantaneous joy in our part of the room. Opal and Raisin jump up and down and squeal. Raisin bows and thanks everyone as he goes up to attack Susan with the biggest hug his skinny body can give.

I'm happy (for them) and sad (for me and especially Cynthia). Opal and Raisin are headed to FIT in the fall with ten thousand dollars of scholarship and clothing line money in their hands. I know Raisin needs the cash, but it's too bad filthy rich Opal gets it. What I'm really envious of are their internships. At least the dress that I helped them drape has been selected for the evening wear section on Floor Two, where the teenage fashionistas shop for the prom. It should be on racks in one month.

Cynthia cusses up a storm, something I've never imagined she could even do. She nudges me, "What did *you* do?"

"I promise I will make it up to you," I say. "We're good. You know that. It's not about this contest anymore. We can think bigger. Will you shop Breakfast around to the boutiques with me?"

She huffs and nods. And then she asks it again:

"Who are you?"

This time, I tell her. I tell her my name is Junebug. I tell her where I'm from. And I tell her that just because my name isn't Cat Zappe doesn't mean the things I did or made as Cat Zappe were a lie. Cat's dresses are still my dresses. Cat's dreams are still my dreams. And Cat's friends, I hope, are still my friends.

I tell her all this. And then, when Raisin and Opal get back, I tell them. Finally, I tell Kera Sahn the whole story.

I know she's disappointed, and still a little in shock. But when I'm done, there's also a little smile on her face.

"I know I should be angry with you," she says. "And if you pull something like this ever again, I will be. But you did what you had to do. In a way, I can respect that. I'm going to assume I can trust you and ask what I wanted to ask all along: I need a TA for my senior level draping class. Interested? You can get your GED this summer, and I know we can get you enrolled for fall."

"Really?" I ask her.

"Really," she says. "After all, it's not like my name is really Kera Sahn. One day I'll tell you what it really is. That's when you'll know I *really* trust you."

Raisin and Opal and their friends are all going out to celebrate, with Cynthia and a lot of our classmates in tow. I don't feel ready to be a part of their celebration yet. My job here is done, and I want to leave. It's time to go home. As sad as I am that I didn't get to win the contest, I'm also a little relieved to be living honestly again. I might have to put Cat Zappe to rest permanently (look at Kera!), but at the very least I need to figure out the real girl underneath.

As I walk out of Bloomingdale's I'm feeling strangely happy, except for one thing:

1. I will be going home with my good news alone.

Despite numerous calls from my new cell phone, I have yet to hear back from a certain clown who certainly must hate me after seeing me leave town with my ex-boyfriend. I told him why I lied about being someone else — because I wanted to be someone new, and I didn't want anyone to be able to find me — and I apologized on his voice mail. I uttered the words, "I'm sorry," at least twice.

I head toward the Bloomingdale's exit doors, the ones that empty out into the subway, and then I hear that deep, tonal voice.

That's when I jump up and down.

I've never been so happy.

"So do you want to know what's in my belly button?"

This is Chapter Thirty-two.

"I'm mad at you." He is so cute in his Shins T-shirt and cowboy boots.

"I owe you Part Four of our agreement. Why does it always feel like I'm saying I'm sorry to you lately?" I give him a hug. He's a little stiff, so I know I'm not totally forgiven.

"Because you didn't tell me much of anything that was the truth. Now I'm going to ask you this: Are you back with your ex-boyfriend?" He isn't playing, not one bit.

"No. Are you back with your ex-girlfriend?" I can play this game, too, even if I already know the answer. Marni is tucked away upstate.

"No."

"Why were you on the bus upstate?"

"I was just riding it to get away — from Marni, from my dad, from everything." He's scratching his head. Clowns are deep. "I like to run, too."

"Then let's go," I say, and I drag him by the arm to Dylan's Candy Bar. It's near Bloomingdale's, so we don't walk too far.

Part Four of what he asked me to do in order to crash in his apartment was take him to this goofy store — a big kid's candy heaven — and buy him all the M&M's he wants.

There are rainbows of them in wall-sized clear cases downstairs.

We throw them into each other's mouths and stop every once and a while to kiss. I'm really looking forward to taking the way I feel right now back to his stainless steel kitchen table. But not now. When we're ready. One day soon.

After an hour and a security guard telling us to "Calm the fritz down," we leave.

"So, does this mean you're coming back to stay with me?" He takes his left hand and moves his golden hair out of his way.

"No freaking way!"

Betsy and I have already dropped off my boxes at the Chelsea Hotel, Room 617.

After all, I'm way too young to live with my new boyfriend.

Part 4

I READ THE NOTE FROM NINA.

This is Chapter Thirty-three.

Dear Baby Jane, Little Junebug,

I'm sorry I left you with so much mess. Take my things, please. Your mother will never appreciate them and love them like you do. Treasure them as you treasured our time together. Ariel will feel guilty for all of it, and she will try to make up with you. Please, darling, make up with her. Never live with her — she will infect you. Stay with Muddy and get your high school diploma properly, as that will give you time to gain the life skills I won't be around to teach you anymore. Be gentle to Muddy, my darling.

Tone down your anger. There is love in this world, especially for you. If you do go off to New York, as I suspect you will, know that you are not ready yet, and it will be a challenge.

But you live for challenges.

Some instructions for successful living in Manhattan:

1. Everything and everyone are interconnected. It's weird how in a big city everything will come together. Don't burn bridges with even one soul — that soul might be able to do you a favor one day.

2. Never, ever, walk fast down a city sidewalk. it's impossible to maintain good posture when hurrying in good shoes. Slow down, my dear, it's more stylish of you.

3. Stay off the A train. it's always been very crowded and unsophisticated. i prefer the C or E.

4. Do not eat the chicken feet in Chinatown, lots of people will dare you to.

5. Never forget to think of me when Breakfast is served at Bloomingdale's all day, every day. i will be there with you, partying on.

Kiss, kiss,

Your Nina